Was that little gi 🔲 P9-APT-079 ...ughter?

It seemed a slim possibility, but one that he couldn't ignore, any more than he could disregard the possibility that he, or some alter ego of his, had a wife.

Into his mind swept the image that had haunted his dreams for the past two nights. An image of Meg Avery. She had the same determined chin as her daughter, along with a tilted nose and full mouth. The eyes were filled with turbulent emotion.

Meg's blouse had shown the outlines of rounded breasts, while her jeans highlighted a slim waist and a very feminine derriere. Could he have made love to such a woman and not remember it?

He needed to find out for sure where he'd been while he was missing.

And he wanted to see Meg Avery again.

Dear Reader,

Welcome to Harlequin American Romance. With your search for satisfying reading in mind, every month Harlequin American Romance aims to offer you a stimulating blend of heartwarming, emotional and deeply romantic stories.

Unexpected arrivals lead to the sweetest of surprises as Harlequin American Romance celebrates the love only a baby can bring, in our brand-new promotion, AMERICAN BABY, which begins this month with Jacqueline Diamond's delightful *Surprise, Doc! You're a Daddy!* After months of searching for her missing husband, Meg Avery finally finds him—only, Dr. Hugh Menton doesn't remember her or their child!

With Valor and Devotion, the latest book in Charlotte Maclay's exciting MEN OF STATION SIX series, is a must-read about a valorous firefighter who rescues an orphaned boy. Will the steadfast bachelor consider becoming a devoted family man after meeting the little boy's pretty social worker? JUST FOR KIDS, Mary Anne Wilson's new miniseries, debuts with *Regarding the Tycoon's Toddler....* This trilogy focuses on a corporate day-care center and the lives and loves of those who work there. And don't miss *The Biological Bond* by Jamie Denton, the dramatic story of a mother who is reunited with the child she'd been forced to give away, when her daughter's adoptive single father seeks her help.

Enjoy this month's offerings, and be sure to return each and every month to Harlequin American Romance!

Wishing you happy reading,

Melissa Jeglinski
Associate Senior Editor
Harlequin American Romance

SURPRISE, DOC!
YOU'RE A DADDY!

Jacqueline Diamond

HARLEQUIN®

TORONTO • NEW YORK • LONDON
AMSTERDAM • PARIS • SYDNEY • HAMBURG
STOCKHOLM • ATHENS • TOKYO • MILAN • MADRID
PRAGUE • WARSAW • BUDAPEST • AUCKLAND

Thanks to Jacqueline Hamilton,
waitress and writer, for her expert advice!

ISBN 0-373-16889-6

SURPRISE, DOC! YOU'RE A DADDY!

Visit us at www.eHarlequin.com

Printed in U.S.A.

ABOUT THE AUTHOR

A former Associated Press reporter, Jacqueline Diamond has written more than fifty books. She lives in Southern California with her husband and two children, and loves to hear from readers at P.O. Box 1315, Brea, CA 92822.

Books by Jacqueline Diamond

HARLEQUIN AMERICAN ROMANCE

HARLEQUIN INTRIGUE

Don't miss any of our special offers. Write to us at the following address for information on our newest releases.

Harlequin Reader Service
U.S.: 3010 Walden Ave., P.O. Box 1325, Buffalo, NY 14269
Canadian: P.O. Box 609, Fort Erie, Ont. L2A 5X3

Dear Reader,

Having babies was both the scariest and the most exciting thing I ever did. Until I was in my late twenties, I wasn't even sure I wanted kids, but after I got married, the maternal alarm clock went off in a big way.

Creating a family didn't turn out to be easy but, as for my hero and heroine, it brought my husband and me closer together. A man's support for his wife and the special bond he forms with his children help to keep love fresh and wonderful over the years.

My heroine knows that, even when her husband disappears, his love for his daughter will someday reunite them. There is nothing stronger in this life than the bond of a parent with a child.

Warmly,

Jacqueline Diamond

Jacqueline Diamond

Chapter One

Meg Avery twisted in her seat to peek at the baby in the back seat. Cradled in her carrier, tiny Dana slept like an angel.

"Has she grown any more toes in the thirty seconds since the last time you checked?" teased her husband Joe from behind the wheel.

Reassured, Meg settled into place. "Babies can get tangled up, or scared or—well, who knows?" Of course, that hadn't happened. If it did, she had a feeling Joe would know about it before she did.

He had formed an almost mystical bond with their daughter from the moment of her birth a month ago. Maybe it was because, after Meg suffered pains two weeks early and delayed going to the hospital because she thought it was false labor, Joe had ended up delivering Dana himself.

A doctor couldn't have done a better job, the paramedics said when they arrived. Ever since, Joe had been the first one to get up and attend to Dana during the night and whenever he was home.

Meg turned her attention to the freeway ahead of her. Through the windshield of her aging sedan, it unrolled for miles as they bypassed downtown Los Angeles, heading north toward her father's home in Santa Barbara.

Although her dad had had a drinking problem in the past, he was sober now, working as a shoe store manager and eager to meet his first grandchild. Meg looked forward to introducing him to Dana.

She turned around and checked on the baby again. Despite earlier efforts to tame them, wisps of red hair stuck up at odd angles.

"You don't have to keep checking. There's no need to worry as long as you follow a few simple precautions," Joe said, speaking in a formal manner that always puzzled her. For a restaurant worker who, like Meg, had never finished high school, he sometimes talked pretty fancy.

"How would you know? You never had a baby before," she pointed out.

"I'm not sure how I know." He rubbed his forehead as if it hurt.

"You're not getting another headache, are you?" Even though her husband seemed healthy, his recurring headaches made Meg worry that he hadn't fully recovered from his near fatal accident eighteen months ago. "I can drive if you like."

"I'm fine, but we are a little low on gas," Joe said. "I'll pull over at the next off-ramp."

"Good idea." She could rely on Joe to keep track of the gas level the same way he kept track of their finances and every other aspect of their lives. She couldn't understand how he'd once had a reputation for being irresponsible.

While he watched for an exit sign, Meg indulged herself in admiring the man to whom she'd been married for an incredibly happy year.

From the side, she studied his well-shaped nose and strong jaw. The morning light transformed his blond hair into spun gold and, when he turned his head to smile at her, his deep green eyes glowed like emeralds.

Joe Avery would make a perfect prince in a fairy tale. To Meg, that's exactly what he was.

Handsome strangers didn't often wander into Mercy Canyon, the small southern California town where she'd lived most of her life. The few who did paid no attention to waitress Meg O'Flaherty, with her bushy reddish-brown hair and freckled cheeks.

Joe hadn't had much choice, she reflected with a glint of humor.

He'd come west from Franklin, Tennessee, to take a job he'd arranged on the Internet at the Back Door Cafe, where Meg worked. En route, he'd stopped at the beach town of Oceanside, twenty miles away.

While fishing from the pier, he'd fallen off and bashed his head. Lifeguards had searched for half an hour until, some distance away, they found him thrashing in the surf.

It was a good thing he'd left his wallet on the pier, because he didn't remember who he was. In his motel room, police had found the phone number of Meg's boss, Sam Hartman, who'd collected Joe and brought him to Mercy Canyon.

Meg had fallen for Joe on sight and nursed him to health. He'd never regained his memory, although she'd learned plenty about him when she contacted a cousin of his in Tennessee.

She learned that, in the past, Joe had drifted from one job to another, impulsively leaving Tennessee for a post that didn't pay any more than he was already earning. The police suggested he might have been drinking before he tumbled off the pier.

Meg didn't care. She knew from personal observation that her Joe Avery was rock-solid. Maybe, she joked to her friends, a blow to the head wasn't always a bad thing.

Tender and funny and amazingly sexy, Joe had claimed her heart and given her his. After surviving a rough childhood during which she and her younger brother Timmy were shuffled in and out of foster homes, Meg couldn't believe her luck. Regardless of what anyone else might believe, she trusted her husband completely.

He pulled off the freeway and down a ramp to a service station. In the back seat, Dana began fussing.

"She needs a diaper change," Joe said, halting at a gas pump.

"I'll do it." Meg knew her husband was as good at changing diapers as she was, but he needed to fill the tank. "I'll take her inside. This chain of gas stations has great baby facilities."

"Don't spend too much time. I hate having you out of my sight in a strange place." Joe wasn't a controlling person but he'd told her that, since his accident, he felt life was precarious.

"We'll be quick." Meg swung out of the car, grabbed the diaper bag and removed Dana from her infant seat.

She took one last, appreciative glance at her husband as he stood at the pump. His muscular build reminded her that he was, indeed, her protector as well as her best friend.

Across the pavement, a red sports car pulled away

from a pump. When it went by, the woman driver studied Joe with interest.

Look but don't touch, Meg thought. *That man belongs to me.*

JOE'S HEART squeezed as his wife crossed toward the station's mini-mart with their daughter on her shoulder. Those two people meant everything in the world to him.

He had no one else. Heck, he didn't even remember the people he'd worked with back in Franklin. Maybe if he'd had some close family, they might have jogged his memory, but his parents had died a few years earlier and there were no siblings.

He wished someone could fill in the inexplicable gaps, the parts of himself that made no sense. When he delivered his daughter, he'd known exactly what to do, yet, when asked, his cousin back in Tennessee couldn't remember him helping with a birth before.

Well, what difference did it make? He was happy being assistant manager of the Back Door Cafe and happy being married to a woman who laughed a lot, had the warmest heart in the world and drove him crazy in bed.

The automatic shutoff on the pump clicked, prompting Joe to remove the nozzle. He'd been so lost in thought that he hadn't noticed two young men in baggy clothing walking toward him, he realized with a start.

Where had everyone else gone? Despite the freeway traffic roaring along nearby, the station was deserted. From out here, Joe couldn't even see the attendant inside the mini-mart.

The men separated, one heading directly toward him and the other coming around the far side of the car.

Please don't let Meg come out of the station now, he thought with a spurt of alarm.

He would willingly give up his wallet and the car, too. Just so no harm came to his family.

"Can I help you?" Joe asked.

"Yeah." The man closest to him pulled a gun from his gray jacket. "Get in the car."

"Here's the keys." Joe held them out, along with his wallet.

"And leave you to yell your head off?" Gray Jacket swiped the wallet and waggled the gun. "Get in or I'll shoot."

Joe shifted uneasily, trying to figure out what to do.

"Now!"

His buddy, a stocky guy in a blue baseball cap, cut off escape in the other direction. Joe weighed dodging between the gas pumps, but if Meg emerged at the wrong moment, things could turn deadly. "Okay, okay." He got into the driver's seat. Blue Cap swung in beside him while Gray Jacket hopped in back, keeping the gun aimed at Joe's head.

"Move it. Fast! South, toward L.A."

The muzzle pressed into his neck. Joe rolled the car forward.

If only there were a way to leave a message for Meg. He hoped that at least someone had witnessed his abduction, so she would know he hadn't run off.

His cousin in Tennessee had told her how unreliable he was. For all he knew, that might once have been true. But he would never leave Meg.

Blue Cap rifled through the glove compartment, cursing at finding nothing but maps, candy and baby wipes. The men grew angrier when they extracted only a small amount of cash from Joe's wallet.

They were looking for drugs and drug money, he gathered. He hoped they would leave when they couldn't find any.

It made him uneasy to realize how many miles were disappearing between him and Meg. Why didn't the men let him pull over and get out?

As he drove, the Los Angeles freeway system began to seem familiar, which was strange considering that Joe hadn't driven much around here before. Not as far as he knew, anyway.

Finally his captors ordered him to exit the freeway in a central city area full of boarded-up buildings covered with graffiti. Blue Cap and Gray Jacket muttered to each other. "Not here." Although Gray Jacket spoke in a low voice, Joe's hearing was keen. "Some place less public."

"Naw. Around here they won't notice the shots," hissed Blue Cap.

They were going to kill him.

Joe's gut tightened. Why would they want to shoot him? Because he could identify them for a crime that so far had done no serious harm? It seemed a ridiculous reason to take someone's life, but these men obviously didn't care.

He had to get away. Had to get back to Meg, to let her know how much he loved her.

At a yellow light, Joe halted sharply. While the two men were regaining their balance, he thrust open the door and leaped out.

"Hey!" Gray Jacket started to roll down his window. About to run across the street, Joe had to scramble back as a truck sped toward him.

Expecting to hear the crack of a bullet at any moment, he zigzagged around the front of the car. Blue

Cap grabbed the wheel and hit the gas, coming after him.

Joe flung himself over the curb a split second before the car reached it, but he wasn't safe yet. As he ducked into an alley, he heard a gunshot.

Desperately, he flung himself to one side. His foot connected with a slippery patch of sidewalk, some kind of spilled food, and he couldn't check his fall.

Flailing in a desperate attempt to regain control, Joe twisted and toppled off balance. For a suspended moment, he registered the fact that his skull was about to hit the corner of a building.

Blinding pain shot through his head. Vaguely, Joe heard a distant siren and the screech of tires as the carjackers fled. Then darkness closed in.

"EVEN WITH the recent advances in imaging technology, there's still a lot we don't know about brain damage," a voice said somewhere in the stratosphere.

A throbbing ache kept his eyes shut. He inhaled the scent of antiseptic and heard a familiar blur of noises: doctors being paged on an intercom, carts jouncing out in a hallway.

"This fresh injury on top of the old one, how is it going to affect his memory?" asked a woman's dry voice.

He recognized the sound, but he couldn't place her. A faint image came into his mind of a rounded face with a charming touch of freckles.

Someone leaned over him. He squinted up through the harsh light.

The face belonged to a woman in her sixties, with wavy silver hair and hazel eyes. Instinctively, his mouth formed the name, "Mom."

His parents were dead. That's what people said in…where?

He tried to recapture the name of the town, or the face he'd visualized earlier. It seemed terribly important, but all he could see was his mother's startled expression.

"He's awake!" she cried. "Hugh's awake!"

Hugh. He rose on a warm cloud of relief. Of course, his name was Hugh, and he'd just come out of an immense black hole. The last thing he remembered was struggling to breathe through shattering waves of cold water.

He'd been sailing with his friend Rick when the boat overturned in the wake of a cabin cruiser. "How's Rick?" Hugh asked thickly.

"Oh, thank God!" his mother cried. "He can speak!" She squeezed his hand. "We'll talk about Rick later."

Something was wrong, he gathered, but couldn't figure out what. Was he worried about Rick or something else?

Impossible to concentrate.

Whatever was nagging at him, he couldn't deal with it now, and he didn't have to. He was safe, in a place where he belonged.

After all, where should a doctor feel more at home than in a hospital?

HOURS LATER, Meg sat drinking tea across the table from her father in his Santa Barbara home. She was still trembling with disbelief.

The events of the day had passed in a nightmarish glare of unreality. Coming out of the gas station to find no sign of her husband. Calling the police, answering endless questions, listening to speculation about how and why Joe had disappeared.

"Somebody must have forced him," she kept saying, but no witnesses could be found. Zack O'Flaherty had driven down when she called and waited for her, clumsily offering to help with Dana, tactfully refraining from voicing the suspicions Meg knew he must feel. She would always be grateful that, at this time of need, her father had come through for her.

The phone rang, startling her so badly she spilled tea on the table.

"I'll get it." With his thin face and pouchy eyes, Zack looked older than his forty-five years, but he walked to the phone with a steady gait.

Meg couldn't bring herself to look at Dana, sleeping nearby in a crib borrowed from a neighbor. What if the police had found Joe's body? What if her little girl had to grow up without a father?

"Yes, I see. Where—? Was there any sign—? I understand. Thank you, officer." Gently, Zack put down the phone.

He isn't dead. If he were, Dad would have asked about claiming the body. Meg managed to breathe again.

"They found your car at a train depot in Los Angeles." Her father resumed his seat across from her. "It was ransacked, but that might have happened after it was abandoned."

"A train depot?" she repeated, trying to derive some useful information from this development.

"They didn't find any blood in the car or nearby," Zack went on. "And no bodies…no injured men have been reported near freeways. For now, Joe's classified as a missing person."

"He was kidnapped!" Meg said.

"I don't doubt it, honey." Her father covered her hand with his. "He had no reason to run off. Even if he suffered some kind of panic attack, he'll come back."

"He didn't leave of his own free will," she said. "I know that, Dad."

"I'm sure you're right."

He couldn't be sure, though, Meg thought. No one could, except her, because no one else knew Joe so well.

A gurgle from the crib drew her attention, and she walked over to monitor the baby. Her daughter wiggled beneath the blanket, then settled back with a blissful sigh.

Joe wouldn't leave her and Dana. Wherever he was, whatever had happened to him, his connection to his wife and daughter would bring him home.

Meg would never stop searching for her husband or believing in him. No matter how long it took.

Chapter Two

Two years later...

Through the tinted window of the high-rise office building, Dr. Hugh Menton stared down over the sun-drenched vista of West Los Angeles. Below, expensive cars navigated the street between sleek modern structures.

He ought to be thrilled that he and his brother could afford a suite in such a prestigious area. Once, being pediatrician to the children of celebrities and business tycoons had been everything he'd hoped for.

Yet, even though he'd outwardly recovered from the still mysterious loss of a year and a half of his life, and even though he'd regained his medical skills, Hugh didn't feel right working here, catering to the rich.

His mouth twisting with disappointment, he turned and tossed the morning mail onto his gleaming oak desk. There was no response yet to his application to take part in a research project working with poor children. He'd hoped to hear from Pacific West Coast University Medical Center by now, since the Whole Child Project started next month, in October.

"You know, the reason you didn't get your letter is

that I've been stealing your mail and burning it,'' said a tenor voice from the hallway.

Hugh looked up with a grin. "Sure you have."

"You'll get tired of playing Dr. Schweitzer," warned his brother. Despite the teasing tone, there was a glint of worry in his green eyes, so much like Hugh's.

Although at thirty-seven Andrew was only two years Hugh's elder, he played the role of senior partner to the hilt. That might be partly because, with his shorter, stockier build and brown hair, he more closely resembled their late father, Frederick Menton, a legendary physician.

And, Hugh reminded himself, Andrew had had to assume the entire responsibility for their joint practice during his own disappearance. "I hope you know that I'd stay here with you if I could. But ever since I got back, I've been restless."

"I've noticed." His brother fiddled with the stethoscope around his neck. "Regardless of how well your injuries have healed, you shouldn't trust these impulses, bro. This isn't like you. You used to enjoy the good life."

Maybe he was right. Hugh couldn't account, rationally, for the sense of incompleteness that had dogged him since his return.

As far as anyone could tell, he must have spent that year and a half as a drifter. He'd disappeared at sea off Oceanside and been found unconscious nearly eighteen months later in Los Angeles, with a fresh head wound and no identification. In between, there wasn't a clue where he'd been.

The only thing Hugh knew for certain was that the experience had changed him. Once ambitious for prestige and material success, he now longed to do some-

thing meaningful with his life. And for an emotional
release that he couldn't name.

If only he knew what had happened during that lost
time!

"As for my leaving, it may be a moot point," he
told his brother. "I haven't heard from the project, so
it doesn't look like I'm going anywhere."

"Good." Andrew checked his watch. "No wonder
Helen isn't bugging us. It's time for lunch."

Helen Nguyen was their nurse and, with patients
prepped in the examining rooms, would never have al-
lowed them to chat for so long. However, no appointments were scheduled between noon and 1:00 p.m.

"Where shall we go?" Hugh asked. Every Wednesday, the two of them lunched at one of the many restaurants in the area.

Once or twice, he'd had in inexplicable urge to point
out to a waiter when he noticed an uncleared table or
a messy front counter. It made him wonder whether he
might have worked in a restaurant while he was gone,
but that didn't give him much to go on.

Chelsea Byers, their receptionist, appeared behind
Andrew, pushing back a strand of her newly dyed ma-
roon hair. "Excuse me." They both turned toward her.
"There's a woman here without an appointment."

"Tell her to make one for later," Andrew said.

"We're full all afternoon, and she says she's driven
a long ways." Chelsea bounced a little, as if she were
dancing at one of the trendy nightclubs she often mentioned. "Her little girl has an ear infection."

"If she comes back after lunch, I'll work her in,"
Hugh said. "Have we seen her before?"

The receptionist shook her head, raising an odd-
colored cloud. "She doesn't have insurance, either."

"Oh, for heaven's sake!" Andrew snapped. "This isn't the welfare office. Where's Sandy?" Sandy Craven, their office manager, was in charge of making sure bills got paid.

"Sandy already went to lunch. The woman said she can pay cash," Chelsea answered. "I'm sorry. I'll tell her she has to arrange payment with Sandy and then make an appointment."

Annoyance at his brother's high-handed attitude spurred Hugh to intervene. "Never mind. I'll see her now."

It was highly irregular and an imposition on Helen, who would need to weigh the little girl and take a brief medical history. Ear infections hurt, though, and he didn't want the child to suffer.

"Don't wait. Go ahead without me," he told Andrew.

"I'm not hungry." Although clearly disgruntled, his brother accepted defeat without further argument.

It occurred to Hugh that, if he did get the research position, Andrew could find a partner who more closely shared his values, someone like Hugh used to be. Maybe that wouldn't be such a bad thing.

A few minutes later, Helen handed him a chart. "Don't wait," Hugh said. "I'm sorry I used up part of your lunch."

"You might need me," the nurse warned.

"Thanks, but I'll handle whatever comes up." He wasn't too snooty to administer a shot if necessary.

After Helen left, Hugh glanced at the chart. The child's name was Dana Avery, age two years. No surgeries or major medical problems. Mother's name Meg, father's name Joe.

Joe Avery. It had a familiar ring, but he couldn't place the man.

Hugh tapped on the door and stepped into the examining room. A small girl with bright green eyes and Little Orphan Annie red hair sat on the examining table, her hands folded in her lap.

It was the sight of the woman standing beside her that, inexplicably, made Hugh's breath come faster. Despite the well-worn blouse and jeans, despite the frizzy reddish-brown hair pulled into an ungracious ponytail, there was something riveting about her.

She was staring at him, too.

"Hello, I'm Dr. Menton." Hugh extended his hand. Dazed, she shook it.

He wanted to ask why she looked so startled, but it seemed intrusive. Hugh's natural reserve would have held him back even if he hadn't been concerned about professionalism.

"You must be Dana," he told the little girl. "Which ear hurts?" She pointed to the left. The child had delicate features and the same alert expression as her mother, he noticed.

"Are you Daddy?" she asked as he examined the ear.

"Dana!" Meg Avery found her voice at last.

"Mommy, you said…"

"No, honey. I'm sorry, Doctor."

"It's all right." Hugh was accustomed to hearing kids blurt out unexpected remarks. "Young children see any adult male as a daddy. It's a generic category."

"'Generic category.'" Nervously, the woman pushed back a strand of hair. "That's how you used to talk, using those formal words, and I couldn't figure it out!"

"Excuse me?"

"I mean, someone I know talked that way." The woman took a deep breath, as if fighting the urge to say more.

Hugh hoped she wasn't unbalanced. Perhaps Andrew had been right to be wary of a new patient who turned up without an appointment.

"Your daughter does have an infection." Briskly, he reached for his pad. "I'm going to prescribe an antibiotic and a decongestant. Make sure she takes all the antibiotics, and have her rechecked in two weeks. You can take her to her regular pediatrician if you prefer."

Meg bit her lip as she took the slip from his hand. Perhaps money was a problem, Hugh thought.

"If you can't afford to fill the prescription, I have some samples in my desk," he said.

Quickly, she shook her head. "I pay my bills."

"I'm sorry." He hadn't meant to offend her pride. And, instinctively, he knew she had a lot of it.

In fact, he felt as if he knew many things about her. That she laughed infectiously. That she was an easy touch for a friend in trouble, but tough as nails toward anyone who tried to rip her off.

He must be imagining things.

"You really don't recognize me, do you?" Meg asked.

"Not offhand," Hugh said. "Have we met?"

"I don't know." She hesitated, shifting from foot to foot as if unsure whether to ask him another question or bolt from the room.

"Did someone refer you to me?" he asked.

"No. Yes." She gave an apologetic shrug that was inexplicably familiar. "My brother Tim saw your picture in the newspaper. He's a truck driver and he stops in L.A. sometimes.''

Hugh and Andrew had been photographed at a recent medical conference. That didn't explain why this woman would come to see him.

He glanced at the chart. ''You live in Mercy Canyon. Where's that?''

''San Diego County,'' she said. ''It's amazing. You look exactly like him. You talk like him, too.''

An uncomfortable suspicion sprang up inside Hugh. ''Like who?''

Although the recent photo caption didn't mention his earlier disappearance, the newspapers had written it up at the time. The unfortunate result had been several attempts to defraud him.

One man claimed he was owed a large gambling debt, and a couple contended they were due hundreds of dollars in back rent. None of them could produce witnesses or signed documents, and the threat of a police investigation had put an end to their claims.

Now this woman contended she had known someone exactly like him. Maybe she'd stumbled across the information on the Internet and decided to try to squeeze out some money.

Yet she didn't strike Hugh as the manipulative type. Perhaps someone else had put her up to it.

Meg swallowed hard and picked up her daughter. ''You can't have forgotten Dana. You delivered her yourself.''

''I haven't delivered babies since my internship.'' Hugh kept his tone level.

''The paramedics said you were as good as a doctor, and I couldn't figure it out because you didn't even have a high school education. You worked at a cafe, like me." Now that she'd started talking, the words spilled out. "Then you vanished with my car. You left us at a gas station. Doesn't this ring a bell?"

"Mrs. Avery, you're clearly distressed," Hugh said gently. "But I've never seen you before."

"The longer I talk to you, the more sure I am that you're my husband!"

"Your husband?"

She shifted her daughter against her shoulder. "It's so hard…you have to remember, Joe. Wait! I can prove it."

She set the little girl on a chair and fumbled in her purse. From the doorway, Andrew peered in and frowned. "What's going on?"

"He's my husband!" Meg said. "I've been looking everywhere for him."

"You believe my brother is your husband?" Andrew lifted a skeptical eyebrow.

Hugh felt awkward for the woman. She spoke so sincerely and so urgently. And the little girl did resemble him, especially those unusual green eyes.

"Look!" Meg Avery thrust a photograph into his hand.

It was a candid shot of her and a man, both beaming at the camera. The man was the spitting image of Hugh.

"He does resemble me." He passed the picture to Andrew.

His brother glanced at it. "Photographs can be altered. Besides, you can't tell me you married a man without knowing who he was."

"I did know, or I thought I did," Meg said. "Joe was from Tennessee. Right after he got to California, he fell off a pier in Oceanside and nearly drowned, and he lost his memory. He had ID but…'' She stopped in confusion.

"What?" Hugh asked.

"Well…" She spoke hesitantly. "After he vanished, I remembered little things. Like that the picture on his driver's license was a poor resemblance. And it had his height wrong, too."

Andrew regarded the woman scornfully. "Let me see if I get this right. You think my brother—a respected pediatrician—stole someone's ID, married you and then fled? Oh, sure. It happens all the time."

"Wait a minute," Hugh said. "Neither of us knows what I did while I had amnesia. I was missing for quite a while."

"When?" Meg asked.

"I turned up two years ago."

"That's when Joe left me!" she said. "I can show you the police report."

Her story wasn't as far-fetched as it might seem, Hugh had to admit. He'd disappeared at sea in the accident that killed his friend Rick. Could he have washed up and been mistaken for another accident victim?

On the other hand, if someone had invented this tale, he or she had cleverly woven in the well-publicized details. And chosen a child the right age to fit the timing.

"You're saying that this is my daughter?" Now Hugh understood why the little girl had called him Daddy. If she'd been deliberately lied to as part of a scheme, it had been a cruel thing to do.

"She is yours," Meg said. "Can't you see she's got your eyes?"

"How do we even know she belongs to you?" Andrew said. "You could have borrowed her to pull a scam."

Hugh wanted to kick his brother. Whatever Andrew's opinion of the woman, he shouldn't speak so harshly in front of the little girl. "The whole question can be resolved by a DNA test," he said quietly.

This was the point at which he expected Meg to feign outrage. With her unruly hair and flashing amber eyes, she could make a great show of being offended.

Of course, she'd never really had a chance of conning him. A doctor wouldn't buy a story like hers without proof, but this woman and whoever had encouraged her might be too unsophisticated to realize that.

She visibly fought to subdue the anger smoldering in her gaze. "All right. What do you need? A blood sample?"

Her agreement startled Hugh. Maybe she honestly believed him to be her missing husband.

"That would suffice." He turned to Andrew. "Would you draw blood for us?"

"You're joking, right?" said his brother. "You're not going to dignify this nonsense by submitting to a test!"

Hugh supposed it was *insulting* to have to go to such lengths to defend himself. He might have withdrawn his offer, except for the tears trembling on the little girl's lashes.

The grown-ups' arguing clearly had upset her. He'd always been empathetic toward children, and this girl's wistfulness touched him deeply.

"What harm can it do? And it will resolve the matter completely." To Meg, he said, "It'll take about a week to get the results."

"I can wait." While Andrew went to find syringes,

Hugh rolled up his sleeve and swabbed his arm with alcohol. He did the same for Dana, while explaining gently that it would hurt a little but was for a good cause.

She believed him instantly. As he leaned close, he inhaled her scent, a blend of baby powder and freshness. The aroma brought a scene vividly to mind.

It was a small room, patchily decorated with flowered curtains and a Minnie Mouse poster. A woman with bushy red hair sat in a rocking chair, nursing a baby.

Maybe it was a scene from a movie, except that it had been summoned to mind by a scent, and movies didn't have scents. As for Meg's hair, his mind might be filling in details from the present, Hugh told himself.

"What?" the woman asked. "Are you remembering something?"

Her face was close to his, the eyes wide, the lips parted. Hugh got a sudden urge to kiss the freckles on her nose. He pulled back.

"No. I haven't eaten lunch yet. I get distracted when I don't eat."

"I know," she said. "You always carried mints for between meals."

There was a roll of mints in his coat pocket right now. Hugh wondered if she had seen the bulge and guessed at its cause. If so, she was very sharp.

Andrew returned with the equipment. Expressionlessly, he drew blood while Meg hovered over her daughter. The little girl winced but didn't cry out. After he finished, Meg handed Hugh a scrap of paper with a phone number. "Please call me when the results come in."

"Our lawyer will call you," Andrew said.

"She's either his daughter or she isn't!" the woman answered. "If she is, that proves he's my husband. I don't see why anyone needs a lawyer."

"If by some bizarre chance you did manage to snare my brother while he wasn't in his right mind, it isn't legal," Andrew said. "You admitted he was using a false ID. You're married to someone who doesn't exist."

"I—" She stared at him in distress. "I never thought of that."

Her mouth trembled as if she might cry. Before any tears could fall, she gathered her daughter and left.

Once her footsteps had faded away, Andrew said, "You don't believe a word of this, do you?"

"I can't dismiss it out of hand." Hugh's skin tingled with the memory of the woman's nearness. He couldn't explain why he felt such a powerful response to a stranger, and yet it was hard to imagine that the two of them had anything in common.

Except, possibly, for one very sweet little girl.

"We should get the results by next Wednesday," Andrew said. "Until then, put her out of your mind."

Hugh wondered if that was possible.

Chapter Three

On the long drive back to Mercy Canyon, Meg battled annoyance and embarrassment as she mentally replayed her meeting with the two doctors. Fortunately, her much-repaired old car rattled along steadily, although the radio was broken and she had to keep the window down to cool the interior.

The brother—Andrew Menton, she remembered from seeing his name on the door—had made her feel sleazy. As for Hugh Menton, he was her Joe right down to his fancy vocabulary and the small scar on his temple. His reserved manner and even temper matched the man she knew, as well.

Meg had instantly recognized the masculine timbre of his voice and the endearing way he ducked his head. When he came close, she'd caught a whiff of the man who'd thrilled her every time he held her. The man she knew with every inch of her body.

Yet he was a complete stranger.

Joe had been an ordinary working guy, blue-collar like her. A man who went bowling with friends and shared the trailer she'd bought with her hard-earned money.

It was doubtful that Dr. Hugh Menton had ever set

foot in a trailer. Not unless he'd conked his head and completely lost his marbles, which, when they got the DNA results, was how he would no doubt account for having fathered a child with Meg.

She remembered her first reaction on seeing the newspaper photo, when her brother, Tim, brought it back from L.A. "A doctor?" she'd said. "Look at him in that tuxedo! Come on. My Joe would never rent a tuxedo to go to a dinner."

Sam, the owner of the Back Door Cafe, had peered over her shoulder at the clipping. "He probably owns the tuxedo."

"Can you own one?" Tim asked. "I thought you just rented them for special occasions."

Judy Hartman, Sam's wife, had poured more coffee for a customer before responding, "I bet you could buy one used, after you rented it."

"A doctor wouldn't need to buy a used tuxedo," Sam said.

They'd debated the topic for a few more minutes before new arrivals at the cafe demanded their attention. Looking back, Meg felt her cheeks get hot.

She could imagine the sneer on Andrew Menton's face if he had heard their discussion. Having seen that expensive office with its big fish tank, thick carpet and elaborate play area, she didn't doubt that both doctors owned tuxedoes. Heck, they probably put one on to take out the trash.

She grinned at the image of snobbish Andrew Menton in a tuxedo, carrying a smelly bag of trash. Except that his family must hire servants to do that kind of thing.

She and Hugh lived in different worlds. Unimaginably different.

It was Meg's friends who'd persuaded her to go to L.A. Tim, Sam and Judy all agreed that the man looked like Joe. So did their bowling buddies Ramon and Rosa Mendez.

"What can it hurt?" Rosa had asked. "You need to take Dana to the doctor anyway. So you make an extra long drive and get a good look at the man. If it's not him, say '*hasta la vista,* baby,' and drive away."

"If it is him, he owes you plenty," said Ramon. "Don't get me wrong. I'm not saying you should be greedy. But he's Dana's father."

For her daughter's sake, Meg had finally decided to go. She'd struggled financially these past two years to support herself and a small child. Friends had helped with baby-sitting, Tim and her father had given her what money they could spare, and she'd muddled through.

It hadn't been easy, though, and it would get even harder as Dana grew up. Eventually she would realize that other girls didn't wear homemade clothes or eat macaroni and cheese three nights a week.

With a sigh, Meg remembered Hugh's offer of free antibiotic samples. She'd been too proud to accept it. Now, as she stopped by the local pharmacy to fill the prescription, she winced at the cost.

She'd been planning to buy Dana a tricycle soon. It would have to wait until Christmas. Later, as she turned into the trailer park, Meg couldn't help seeing it with critical eyes. The residences were parked close together, with only space for a few flowers in front. Most people kept their units tidy and so did she, but her paint was chipped and the awning had rust streaks.

A wave of longing rushed over her. She and Joe had

cherished dreams of buying their own home. Nothing elaborate; a modest three-bedroom fixer-upper.

They'd talked about decorating a nursery, and putting a workshop for Joe in the garage. "I want an extra freezer so I can stock up on meat and pizza when they're on sale," Meg had said, relishing the prospect after battling to stuff food into a tiny, overcrowded freezer compartment.

She wanted her Joe back, the man who had shared those dreams. A man who would never have imagined owning a tuxedo or even renting one. He'd worn a plain suit for their wedding, looking heart-stoppingly handsome in the dark fabric.

Meg parked alongside her trailer and lifted Dana from her seat. By the porch, a stray cat who'd been hanging around regarded them with mingled hope and fear. Its fur had a pandalike pattern of black and white.

"Pat kitty!" cried Dana.

"Not right now." Even in September, this far inland the temperatures soared, and Meg was eager to turn on a fan and make iced tea. "Let's go inside."

"Feed kitty?" her daughter asked.

"We shouldn't encourage him," Meg said. "We can't afford a pet."

Inside, the trailer was stifling. She opened the windows and fixed cold drinks.

After the spaciousness of Hugh's office, her home felt cramped. Meg tried not to notice the odds and ends of furniture bought at garage sales.

It wasn't the lack of frills that bothered her. It was the absence of the man she loved. And something else.

As she sank onto the couch, watching Dana play with her favorite dolls, Meg realized what was troubling her.

For two years, she'd refused to give up hope. Even when she saw the doubt in some people's eyes, she'd persisted in believing that Joe loved her and that, when she found him, they would resume their life together.

Now, perhaps, she had found him, but if Hugh Menton was Joe, he wasn't *her* Joe. He might as well live on Jupiter.

Maybe, as Andrew had said, she was in love with someone who didn't exist. For the first time, Meg had to face the possibility that she might never get her husband back.

No LETTER came for Hugh on Thursday or Friday. He put in a call to Dr. Vanessa Archikova, director of the Whole Child Project at Pacific West Coast University, and had to leave a message.

It was not a good sign.

Less than a month remained before the research program started. If they wanted him, surely they'd have notified him by now. There was nothing wrong with the job he had, Hugh reflected as he paused between patients to update his notes. Counseling anxious parents, healing injured or ailing children and referring the rare serious cases to the best specialists were valuable services.

Yet a chasm lurked inside him. If his application were rejected, he needed to find some other way to give meaning to his life.

The Whole Child Project, funded by a private research grant, had been designed by a panel of experts headed by Dr. Archikova. It proposed to use medical personnel, in conjunction with parents and schools, to coordinate the care of a group of poor children in hopes of making a large impact on their futures.

Many of the kids came from homeless families. Others lived in foster homes. Most had borderline nutritional and behavioral disorders.

Government-run attempts to help them had bogged down in paperwork and politics. The Whole Child Project was their last chance.

It would be thrilling to make a difference for those kids, Hugh thought. He'd always loved children. Maybe that was why he couldn't stop thinking about one particular little girl with flaming red hair and elfin features.

Was she really his daughter? It seemed a slim possibility, but one he couldn't ignore, any more than he could disregard the possibility that he, or some alter ego of his, had a wife. Into his mind swept the image that had haunted his dreams for the past two nights. An image of Meg Avery.

She had the same determined chin as her daughter, along with a tilted nose and full mouth. The eyes were filled with turbulent emotion.

Her blouse had shown the outlines of rounded breasts, while her jeans highlighted a slim waist and a very feminine derriere. If she'd been his wife, they must have spent many nights together. Luscious nights tangling between the sheets, steaming up the bedroom.

Had they really lain together, both of them naked and aroused? Could he have made love to such a woman and not remember it?

"You're a million miles away." Helen Nguyen smiled as she passed Hugh in the inner corridor between examining rooms. It was midafternoon, and the after-school crowd of patients would soon stream in. "Daydreaming about the weekend?"

"Trying to plan my future," he said. "It's hard to move forward when you don't understand the past."

"Do you mean that woman who was here Wednesday?" Helen asked. "Andrew told me she claims to be your wife."

Petite and dark-haired, the nurse twinkled up at him. She'd been a big help in making Hugh feel at home when he came back to work, and she'd become a good friend.

Last February, he'd joined her and her husband in celebrating Tet, the Vietnamese New Year, at a festival in Orange County. It was an adventure that the old, stuffy Hugh might have passed up. "I'm not sure what to believe," he admitted. "What did you think of her?"

Helen paused to reflect. "She was a little nervous. Now I understand why. You know, I liked her. And the child, well, those eyes do look like yours and Andrew's."

"I need to know where I was all that time," Hugh said. "With such a gap in my self-knowledge, any decision I make about the future might be flawed."

"What? A great and mighty doctor, admit to weakness?" teased Helen. "While I recover from my shock, please excuse me to see to a patient."

"By all means." Amused, Hugh picked up a chart and went to examine a little boy who'd twisted his ankle.

Musings about the past dogged him for the rest of the day. He needed to find out for sure where he'd been while he was missing.

And he wanted to see Meg Avery again.

His common sense told him to wait until the DNA

results came back. That she might be a trickster, or a nutcase.

Still, he had no plans for the weekend. The palatial Hollywood Hills home he shared with his mother and with Andrew's family would be empty tomorrow.

Andrew and his wife, Cindi, were taking their children to their vacation cottage in Redondo Beach. Grace Menton, who headed a charitable committee that was sponsoring a dinner and evening at the opera, planned to work hard behind the scenes at that event.

Hugh would be alone. What harm could it do to drive by Mercy Canyon and see where Meg and Dana Avery lived?

Hugh could almost hear his brother warning of possible legal entanglements. There was no need to announce his presence or get involved in any way, however.

As he finished his notes for the evening, he knew he was going to make the trip. If nothing else, it might help him get this woman out of his system.

"NO, I'M NOT SURE it's him. I mean, I *was* sure at first, but every day I wonder if I wasn't imagining the resemblance," Meg admitted as she awaited her turn at the bowling alley on Saturday.

"It sure looked like Joe in the picture," said Rosa Mendez, blowing the steam off her cup of coffee. In her early forties, she maintained a trim figure in shorts and a sleeveless blouse.

"Well, I've got an old picture of me that looks like Dolly Parton," said Judy Hartman. Away from work, she wore her long blond hair full and curly, with the help of regular visits to Rosa's beauty salon. "That doesn't mean I can sing."

"That doctor isn't Joe," Ramon said from his seat at the scoring table. "Come on. Some big-shot pediatrician worked at the cafe for a year and a half? I don't believe it."

"Anybody notice I just got a spare?" asked Sam Hartman, rejoining them.

"Way to go!" cheered Ramon.

As on most Saturdays, the group of friends had met at 11:00 a.m. at Mercy Lanes, next to the Back Door Cafe. The Hartmans were the best players, but everyone enjoyed the fun and the companionship.

The youngsters with them—the Hartmans' sixteen-year-old son and the Mendezes' three kids, who ranged from seventeen to twenty-one—formed their own group a few lanes away. Otherwise, the alley was empty except for a cluster of people around the video-games in back.

"If you're not sure it's him, what are you going to do?" Judy asked Meg.

"She's going to play. It's her turn." Sam reached for his soft drink.

Glad to escape Judy's question, Meg hurried to retrieve her ball. She didn't know what she was going to do about Hugh Menton. She almost hoped the DNA test came back negative so she wouldn't have to decide.

Life without Joe had settled into a comfortable if sometimes lonely pattern. She enjoyed times like today, when she could chitchat and bowl while Dana played at their next-door neighbor's trailer.

If Hugh did turn out to be Joe, he might disrupt her entire existence. While he wasn't likely to claim Meg as his wife, he might insist on spending time with Dana. Maybe even want her to live with him.

Grimly, she stared at the lane in front of her. No way would she give up her daughter! Angrily, Meg rolled the ball.

With a whump, it hit the gutter. Whistles and catcalls erupted behind her.

"Get your mind out of the gutter, girl!" called Rosa.

Darn. The man was messing with her bowling game. When the ball came back, Meg focused, started forward and rolled again.

Clean and sure, the ball flew down the lane and smashed into the pins. With a clatter, they shot in all directions. Of the few that remained, several wobbled and dropped at the last minute, leaving two standing.

"Too bad you didn't get your act together the first time," Ramon said as she returned. "You could have hit a spare."

"They're too far apart," Meg said. "I'd never have made it."

"That's your problem, Meg," advised Sam as his wife went to bowl. "You don't give yourself enough credit."

"Don't mention credit." She shuddered. No matter how hard she tried to pay down her charge card, the balance always hovered near her limit. The mobile home park fee, food and baby-sitting ate most of her income.

"I'll tell you what," Rosa said. "I'll give you a freebie. Come by the salon this afternoon and I'll cut your hair. It'll look cute."

Rosa had been itching to get her hands on Meg's mane for years. Without her bushy hair, though, Meg wouldn't feel like herself. "No, thanks. I'm taking Dana swimming."

The local community center pool cost a dollar per

person, with kids under five free. It was one of the few treats they could afford.

Judy hit a strike, and whooped with delight at besting her husband this round. After that, the players concentrated on their games, and Meg finished with a respectable score.

She felt better by the time she left. Life in Mercy Canyon was safe and solid.

Even if he turned out to be Joe, Hugh Menton might never appreciate this town as he once had. Heck, he'd probably never bother to visit here.

Meg didn't care. She knew where she belonged, and nothing could change that.

To REACH Mercy Canyon, Hugh drove his luxury sedan on narrow, winding back roads. He hadn't believed two-lane highways existed anymore in the age of carpool lanes and ever-wider freeways.

For a long stretch after he left the tightly packed developments of the coastal zone, he saw only a few isolated shacks and passed a mere handful of cars. Urban sprawl hadn't reached this part of San Diego County.

In September, the height of the dry season, a scattering of dusty trees drooped in a rocky canyon filled with dry grasses and flowers. The area didn't look familiar. Had he truly lived here for a year and a half?

As he descended from a slope, a sign alerted Hugh that he was entering the town of Mercy Canyon. He didn't see anything until he rounded a rock outcropping and suddenly, below him, spread the community where he might have spent his lost months. Wanting time to collect his impressions, he stopped the car on the shoulder.

From this rise, he made out clusters of stores, an elementary school, a church, a couple of modest-size light-industrial buildings and numerous houses. There was a trailer park at the far end of town.

Hoping the scents would jog his memory, Hugh rolled down the window. Hot air blasted into his air-conditioned cocoon.

As he'd expected, it carried the smells of eucalyptus and desert plants. For a split second, he remembered coming out of a cool building into the same heated air.

He was emerging from a church with a woman at his side. People lined the walkway, blowing soap bubbles. Could it be his own wedding?

Although Hugh had come here in search of the past, this possibility disturbed him. It was alarming to think that he might really have been a different person and lived a different life for so many months.

He knew of course that he'd been *somewhere* during his absence. Yet couldn't the time have passed, as his family wanted to believe, in a succession of meaningless days of panhandling and sleeping in shelters?

On the other hand, before he was released from the hospital, Hugh's doctor had remarked on what good shape he was in, aside from the head injury. He hadn't been starving on the streets.

Maybe Meg's story was true. He might be a husband and father. Hugh's breath caught in his throat. So much for the rationalization that he could drive by Mercy Canyon and leave without seeing the Averys.

He'd brought Meg's address. He could see the park distantly from here, neat rows of mobile homes glinting in the sunlight.

At the prospect of visiting what might be his old home, a twinge of fear ran through Hugh. What was he afraid of, that he would stumble into an unpleasant trap of his own making? Or that he would discover he'd once lived in paradise and couldn't go back again?

There was no sense in delaying the inevitable. After rolling up the window, he turned on the ignition and started forward.

Chapter Four

Halfway through the town of Mercy Canyon, Hugh got a prickly sensation down his back. He knew this place as if from a dream.

The strip mall to one side of the road looked like a thousand others in Southern California. Yet he felt a twinge of recognition as he parked in front of a coffee shop called the Back Door Cafe.

Handwritten specials and flyers for local school fundraisers plastered the window, while the interior was hidden behind a lopsided Venetian blind. A thought came to him: *The slats always pull crookedly. You'd think they'd have fixed them by now.*

To one side sat a bowling alley. On the other, a bilingual video store featured posters of newly released films in Spanish and English.

At the end of the mall lay a salon called Rosa's Beauty Spot. Oddly, he knew that Rosa was married to the owner of the video store.

He had been here before.

Hugh sat in his car, staring at the cafe. He'd had flashes of memory before, but none had ever been tied to a particular place. The clatter of dishes in a restaurant, the cry of a baby, the scent of old-fashioned perfume would snatch him momentarily from his reality, and then drop him right back into it.

His heart raced with an emotion akin to fear. There was no reason for alarm, yet it disturbed him to realize that he might be about to confront an unknown part of himself.

Most likely, he'd psyched himself to believe he'd once worked here because of what Meg had said, Hugh thought sternly. Annoyed at himself for indulging in useless worry, he got out, crossed the walkway and pushed open the cafe door.

The smell of coffee and frying hamburgers greeted him, familiar as a friend's face. Still, who hadn't smelled coffee and hamburgers before?

To his left stretched a counter where a grizzled man in a cowboy hat sat drinking coffee. To his right lay a row of booths, one of which held a family of four. In the back, past an open archway, sunlight from side windows streamed into a large room filled with tables and booths.

"Can I help you?" A young Hispanic man behind the counter regarded Hugh with impersonal friendliness that rapidly changed to confusion. "Say, man, you look familiar."

"Have you worked here long?"

"About a year." The fellow was no older than twenty, Hugh guessed. "I'm the assistant manager, Miguel Mendez." He extended his hand.

Hugh shook it. "I'm Dr. Hugh Menton." He hadn't meant to throw in his title, but it slipped out.

"You're a doctor?"

"Pediatrician." Hugh decided to risk another question. "Does Meg Avery work here?"

"Sure."

A tall, blond waitress came out of the kitchen hefting a tray of burgers, fries and drinks. When she saw Hugh, she stopped dead.

"Doggone you, Joe Avery!" she said. "What do you mean disappearing and then turning up like this? Does Meg know you're here?"

"I thought you looked familiar," Miguel said. "What's this doctor business, man?"

Hugh wondered if he'd fallen asleep. This felt like one of those dreams in which he found himself on stage, expected to enact a role he hadn't learned. Or in an operating room, about to perform surgery on an organ he'd never heard of.

"You think I look like Joe Avery?" he asked.

"Do I think you look like him?" The woman uttered an unladylike snort. "Come on, Joe, I worked with you for a year and a half."

"You served me coffee every morning," confirmed the grizzled man at the counter. "So you became a doctor? That's pretty smart."

"You can't become a doctor in two years," said Miguel. "I don't think so, anyway."

"Sam!" yelled the waitress. "Get out here right now!"

Through the swinging door barreled a large, beefy man wearing a white apron and holding a fire extinguisher. "What's going on?"

"You can put that away. There's no fire, just a prodigal son," said his wife.

His wife. Her name's Julie...no, Judy. Hugh stared at them both. He knew these people, or half knew them.

"Do you recognize me?" he asked.

"Joe Avery! I'll be doggoned!" Sam frowned as he

studied Hugh. "You got a new scar on your forehead. Where'd that come from?"

"I hit my head on the side of a building, so the police tell me," he said.

"Get this. Joe told Miguel he's a doctor," Judy said.

"According to Meg, he *is* a doctor, remember?" Sam said. "You saw the clipping."

"Doctors don't serve coffee in restaurants," said the grizzled man. "Although one time when you spilled some on my hand, you bandaged it real nice. I'm Vinnie Vesputo. Remember me?"

"I wish I did," Hugh said.

The mother in the booth waved her hand. "Could we have our food, please?"

"Sorry!" Judy carried the tray to them.

"Would you mind showing us some ID?" Sam asked Hugh. "It might make things a little clearer."

"Yeah. I'm kind of confused," Miguel said.

"You're not the only one." Hugh took out his wallet and showed them the driver's license. Judy came over and scrutinized it, finally shrugging as she absorbed the fact that he was indeed Hugh Menton, M.D. "I've got a year and a half missing from my past. To walk in here and meet people who know me feels strange."

"You don't recognize us?" Sam sounded hurt. "Not at all?"

This was a good man, Hugh knew. A man who'd helped him when he was hurt. "You took care of me at one point, didn't you?"

"Hauled you back from Oceanside like a drowned rat and held your job until you got over your pneumonia," he said. "So that really was you that Meg went to see in Los Angeles?"

"It was indeed."

"Quite a shock for both of you, huh?"

"You might say that. In fact, you could definitely say that." Hugh was surprised at how easily he fell into conversation with Sam. Although superficially they had nothing in common, he liked the fellow.

More people entered the cafe, and Judy went to show them to a table. At Sam's gesture, Hugh followed him through swinging doors into the kitchen.

Metallic counters and sinks gleamed on both sides of the narrow room. Through a slim horizontal opening, they could see the counter area.

"We can talk better in here. Besides, I've got work to do," Sam said. "Have a seat, Doc."

Hugh perched on a stool. "Tell me about myself. What I was like."

"Incompetent, at first." Sam lifted a metal basket of French fries from boiling fat, let it drain and set it under a warmer. "But careful. Man, the first time you made coffee, it was like you were measuring it for a science experiment."

"So that's where I learned to make coffee." Hugh had startled his office staff one morning when he arrived early by taking care of that task for the first time. He'd been puzzled when he discovered that he knew instinctively what to do.

"After a while, you loosened up," Sam said. "Cracked jokes. Sneaked in beer when we were working late. Talked me into driving all the way to San Diego to look at a panda in the zoo. You were the first guy I ever met who's as crazy as I am."

"Me?" *Crazy* was not an adjective anyone would apply to the cautious Hugh Menton.

Hugh had kept his nose to the grindstone through medical school, conscious of the need to live up to his legendary father's reputation and to Andrew's excellent record. Looking back, he supposed the other students had found his perfectionism annoying.

"I don't suppose you'd consider coming back?" Sam asked wistfully. "Miguel's a nice kid but he ought to go to college. Besides, he's not very interesting to talk to."

"I'm afraid I can't," Hugh said. "Although I appreciate the offer."

"You're really a doctor?" Sam persisted. "It's not just some mail-order Ph.D.?"

"U.C.L.A. Medical School," Hugh said. "With a residency in pediatrics."

"How'd you end up as Joe Avery, anyway?" Sam asked.

Hugh explained about the capsized boat, Rick's death and how he'd apparently washed ashore. "I suppose it happened right when the real Joe Avery fell off the pier," he said.

"So he must be dead?" Sam asked.

"My brother says that, shortly after I disappeared, he was contacted about an unidentified drowning victim in Oceanside. Of course, it wasn't me, and by then Joe was no longer considered missing. Yesterday, I called the police to suggest they compare the DNA to that of the real Joe Avery."

"I'm glad. The guy deserves to rest in peace." Sam removed some hamburger patties from a freezer.

Hugh's original plan to view the town and slip away unnoticed would be impossible now that he'd been recognized. Besides, he was in no hurry to leave. "Is Meg working today?"

"Not till tonight. She took Dana to the community

pool," Sam said. "How are things between you two, anyway?"

"Unsettled."

"Meg's a good woman. You should..." The cook broke off as his wife thrust an order at him through the narrow aperture.

It was an informal setup, Hugh noted, based on his observation of coffee shops he'd patronized over the years. "You ought to enlarge that window and put in some warmers so you could set the trays there. Buy one of those round holders that she could clip the orders to."

"Yeah, like you never said that before!" Sam shook his head. "I guess you don't remember saying it, do you?"

"I'm afraid not," Hugh said. "Whatever advice I gave you, I'm sure it was right on target."

"Man, you haven't changed! Still as cocky as ever."

They grinned at each other. A strange but pleasant sensation rippled through Hugh. A sense of belonging.

He gave himself a mental shake. "I'd like to find Meg. Where's the pool she took Dana to?"

"Go two blocks south and turn right on Arroyo Grande," Sam said.

"Thanks." A few minutes later, Hugh was on his way.

DANA HAD MADE a new friend in the wading pool, a little boy with a plastic boat. They spent half an hour pretend-racing it from side to side, weaving between the other children.

Meg sunbathed in her bikini. Although she occasionally greeted an old friend en route to the larger pool nearby, she felt very much alone. In the kiddie section, most of the moms were accompanied by their husbands, except for one young woman who'd come with her mother.

Keeping a cautious eye on Dana, Meg leaned back in the plastic lounge chair and imagined how Corinne O'Flaherty would have doted on a granddaughter.

Thinking of her mother was like picturing two entirely different people. One warm and loving, full of fun. The second alternating between deep depression and intense irritability.

Her father's bouts with alcohol hadn't made life any easier. Since his recovery, however, Meg had forgiven him and they'd grown close these last few years.

Tim refused even to speak to the man. He understood that their mother had been a victim of mental illness, but he couldn't extend the same forgiveness to the father who'd abandoned them.

Meg wished Tim could find a woman to make him as happy as Joe Avery had made her. Once he was a father himself, maybe he would soften toward the man who now deeply regretted having failed them. She knew how much she'd matured after experiencing true intimacy with Joe.

Looking up, she squinted against the glare of sunlight. That man walking toward her sure did resemble her husband. It must be a trick of the light, or of her longing.

He had the same graceful stride, straight shoulders and strong arms. The same boyish crease in one cheek that, as always, set her heart pounding.

Despite his modesty, Joe had always had a magnetic presence, and now she noticed how women's heads swiveled to follow him. With an electric jolt, Meg realized it was Hugh Menton.

She straightened on her chaise longue. "What are you doing here?"

He pulled over a plastic chair, checked to make sure it was dry and sat down. Although tailored slacks and a crisp short-sleeved shirt might seem overdressed at a pool, it was the other people who looked underdressed by comparison.

"I dropped by to see the town," he said. "I thought it might jog some memories."

"Remember anything yet?"

Instead of answering, Hugh glanced toward the wading pool. "I could spot Dana a mile away. That hair is amazing."

As always, mention of her daughter made Meg smile. "She comes by it naturally." She shook back her own frizzy cloud until it tickled her shoulders.

"So I see." Hugh regarded her warmly. "I like your hair loose that way."

His appreciation quivered through her. How like Joe to talk about her hair when she was sitting here in a bikini! Unlike most men, he was too much of a gentleman to comment on how the rest of her looked.

That didn't mean he was unaware of her. Sensitized to him as always, Meg noted his speeded-up intake of breath. In response, heat thrilled through her.

She missed him physically as well as emotionally. Missed the hungry probing of his mouth and the way he gently but firmly took command when they made love.

Yet this man remembered none of that. Even if he once had been her husband, he was a stranger now.

"You didn't answer my question," she said. "Does any of this seem familiar?"

"I went by the restaurant." He relaxed as the breeze

ruffled his sandy hair. "Saw Sam and Judy. I'm not sure whether I recognize them or I was responding to suggestion."

There he went again, using high-flown language. "I guess you mean that I put ideas in your head."

"That's right. Not that I'm implying you did it on purpose."

"Two years is a long time for you to be in the dark," she said. "Can't your doctors do anything about this amnesia business?"

"The brain is incredibly complicated and still not fully understood." Hugh watched as Dana and her new friend splashed each other playfully. "My neurologist can't say why I've recovered everything from before my accident but lost that year and a half. He thinks it might be because I reinjured the same area of the brain."

"So the time you spent here could be gone permanently?" Meg asked. "Erased like an old videotape?"

He shot her a startled glance. "That's a good simile."

"A good what?"

"Figure of speech," he said. "The answer is, I was beginning to fear it might be gone forever, but visiting the restaurant today stirred something. Either memories or false memories. Not entirely false, though, I don't think."

Meg had seen a story on TV about people so gullible that they could be persuaded to remember things that had never happened. She supposed that was what he meant by false memories, but surely that wasn't the case with Hugh.

There was another question she ached to ask. A dangerous question, but this seemed as good a time as any.

"Joe—Hugh—is there someone else? Another woman in your life?"

"No. Ever since I got back, I knew there was something missing. Until I figured it out, I wasn't ready to start a new relationship," he said.

Hugh had missed her. A tiny hope lit within Meg.

Maybe he couldn't go back to being the same Joe she'd known, but if he loved her, he might move to Mercy Canyon and practice medicine here. Their lives could continue pretty much as planned.

The security she'd longed for since she was small might still be possible. To have a loving husband here where she belonged, surrounded by old friends, and to have her daughter grow up in such a safe environment, was all Meg wanted.

At the wading pool, the little boy's mother lifted him onto a towel to dry off. Dana climbed out and headed for Meg.

When she spotted Hugh, the little girl's eyes widened. With an expression of pure bliss, she shouted, "Daddy!" and ran to him.

He barely got out of his chair in time to catch her. "Hi, honey." Hugging her, Hugh paid no notice to the water dripping over his clothes.

"My Daddy!" Dana announced to everyone. "Mine!"

When he lifted her, she wrapped herself around him as if she'd known him all her life. "Are you having a good time, sweetie?"

"Us go home!" she cried.

"That's right, we're going home," Hugh said. "Together."

Meg's chest squeezed at seeing her family reunited. "Last one to the parking lot's a cross-eyed gopher!" she said, and grabbed her gear.

Chapter Five

Hugh felt as if he'd been holding this little girl in his arms every day for the past two years. The way she curled against him and the fresh scent of her hair felt utterly familiar.

His daughter. She'd always been with him, even if he hadn't known it.

He'd missed so much of her life. And, without realizing it, he'd missed Meg.

Hugh had wondered at his lack of response to women in the past two years. He'd kept watching for some quality that was missing. An honesty that, he realized now, was an essential part of Meg's appeal.

He loved the way she looked, too, even though she wasn't conventionally beautiful. Walking ahead of him with a towel slung around her shoulders, she glowed with natural sensuality.

He wished he could remember making love to her. How she looked without that bikini….

When they reached Meg's car, he strapped Dana into her child seat. This dented sedan made him uneasy, as if a painful memory were connected with it. He couldn't summon any specifics and wasn't sure he wanted to.

In his own car, Hugh followed Meg through town. He had an urge to shout at every vehicle that approached, "Slow down! Don't hit them!"

He wanted to protect them. It was such a fundamental urge that it bypassed his intellect, which warned that they might not really be his.

The two-car caravan entered the trailer park between a scattering of tall palm trees. Mobile homes crammed the spaces, and a flock of children rode scooters in the narrow roadway.

As Hugh steered carefully between them, he vowed silently that his daughter wouldn't grow up playing in the street. She should have her own yard and a sidewalk where she'd be safe.

Meg stopped at a small unit and, leaning out the car window, waved him to the visitor slots a short distance farther. After parking, Hugh walked back amid the blare of a radio through an open window and the chatter of a TV from another unit.

Meg waited till he reached her before shepherding Dana inside. Following, Hugh found himself wanting to crouch because of the low ceiling, although it wasn't low enough to bean him.

He took in the sprinkling of toys on the floor, the mismatched furniture, the plastic flowers filling a vase on the coffee table. Disappointment darkened his mood. If he'd ever stayed in this place, his brain contained no record of it.

"Did we live here?" he asked.

Meg nodded. "I hoped you might remember."

"I'm sorry."

"Never mind. Excuse me a minute. I've got to help Dana change clothes." She carried the toddler into a bedroom.

Perhaps he really wasn't Joe, Hugh thought. Surely her husband would feel at home in the place where they'd lived.

He certainly wouldn't have forgotten making love to Meg. Eating dinner with her, curling up in bed with her, taking a shower together in the morning. Not if he'd really done those things.

Without thinking, he trailed in Meg's wake and peered into Dana's room. Flowered curtains. An aging rocker. A poster of Minnie Mouse on the wall.

He'd pictured those things when Meg was in his office. This very room. So he *had* been here before!

The clues fit too, Hugh reflected, sorting through them mentally. Rick's sailboat had sunk shortly before the watery rescue of Joe Avery. People at the Back Door Cafe recognized him, and Meg had a police report showing that her husband had vanished the same day Hugh turned up in Los Angeles.

Everything pointed to the likelihood that he had lived in this place and fathered a child. Still, that didn't make it true. As a doctor, Hugh knew that mountains of circumstantial evidence didn't amount to gold-standard proof. Even his own memories might be misleading.

Seeking more clues, he gazed at a couple of photos on the living room wall. There was one of him and Meg with baby Dana, but Hugh, or rather Joe, had his face slightly averted. Another picture showed Meg beside a thin young man with reddish-brown hair like her own.

"That's my brother, Tim," she said, joining him. Changed into a pair of white jeans and a blue-green camp shirt, she smelled of flowers and a trace of chlorine. "I dropped out of school to raise him after our mother died."

"Couldn't your father handle him?"

"Dad had a drinking problem. He wasn't around," she said. "He's been dry for nearly ten years now."

Hugh moved away from the pictures. "Where's Dana?"

"Taking a nap," she said. "Want some coffee?"

"Sure." In the small kitchen, he turned a chair backward and straddled it.

"You always sat that way." She pointed at the floor. "Look."

On the linoleum, two worn patches lay directly beneath Hugh's feet. It gave him an eerie feeling to realize that he, or someone, had sat in exactly this position many times.

"That *is* interesting," he said.

He still didn't recall living in the trailer. Or perhaps he couldn't think straight with Meg sitting across from him, her camp shirt's low V-neck revealing the swell of her breasts. To Hugh's embarrassment, Meg noticed him staring. "Stir any memories?"

"Is that what you're trying to stir?" he teased. "I'm only human, you know."

She gave him a mischievous grin. "You're a doctor. Anatomy isn't supposed to affect you."

"It depends on the circumstances. Shall I treat you as the mother of a patient, or as the mother of my child?"

"That depends on how you see me." Her amber eyes dared him to respond.

"I don't know how I see you," Hugh admitted. "It's hard to trust someone who suddenly appears in my life, no matter how much I want to."

She sighed. "Thank goodness for DNA tests. What if they didn't exist? I'd have to find another way to prove my case."

"How would you do that?" he asked, intrigued.

Meg tossed her mane. "I suppose I could seduce you and hope it reminded you of what we had before. That raises some weird moral issues. I don't even know if you're legally my husband."

"People don't have to be married to make love," he said.

"I did!" Her mouth tightened. "You were the first man I was ever with."

"I'm sorry if I offended you." Hugh reached across the table to cup her hand. He tried to ignore the shiver of desire that ran through him at the contact. "That was a special gift you gave me."

As Meg turned away, he saw a sheen of moisture in her eyes. "I waited a long time for the right man. Who could have believed we'd end up in such a mess?"

"I'm curious about our relationship." Despite a few immature entanglements earlier in life, Hugh had never felt truly close to a woman. Yet during his lost months, he'd evidently fallen in love with Meg and she with him. "How did you know I was the right man?"

"Joe—you—made me laugh," she said.

"Me? I never make anybody laugh except when I trip over my own feet."

"You made me laugh with the way you saw things, like everything was fresh and new and wonderful," she said. "Also, I liked the way you moved."

"I wasn't aware of moving in any particular manner." Although Hugh had been a diver in college and swam laps daily in the family pool, he considered himself a klutz on the dance floor.

"That's because you can't see yourself from the rear," Meg teased.

He ducked his head. "I never thought about the way I walk."

"You're cute when you're embarrassed," she said. "That's the third thing I like."

"Those aren't reasons to fall in love," he protested.

"Why not?"

"They lack substance."

"People don't fall in love with their brains," Meg said.

He supposed she was right. Through his hand curved over hers, Hugh was intensely aware of the softness and warmth of her skin. He noted the quivering freckles across her cheeks and the way the collar of the shirt fell open to bare a vulnerable patch of shoulder.

Sexual attraction wasn't love, but it might be the first step. Besides, what he felt went far beyond the physical.

"I wish I remembered what it was like to be with you." He gave her an apologetic grin. "I'm sure it was spectacular."

"I remember what *you* were like," she retorted, and had the grace to blush. "Now we're both embarrassed."

In the other room, Dana began babbling. Meg excused herself to check on her. When she returned, she stood by the counter. "She was talking in her sleep."

The spell had broken between them, although Hugh felt a residual hum of excitement. He'd never met a woman to whom he responded so strongly. Even if he weren't Joe, he was glad to have discovered Meg.

And Dana. "Have you thought about her future?" he asked. "Your—our—daughter's?"

"What about her future?"

"Surely you don't want her to grow up riding a scooter in the street." He gestured toward the window, through which they could hear children's shouts and the scrape of metal wheels on concrete. "And you want her to get a good education, don't you?"

Meg gripped her mug. "Of course, I want her to graduate from high school."

"Then she should go on to college," Hugh said.

"There's a community college not far away." Meg remained standing. "She could commute and work at the restaurant on weekends."

"I know she isn't even in preschool yet," he said. "But if she's my daughter, Meg, I want more for her. Where I live, the environment is much more challenging...."

He stopped, seeing the determination written on her face. Apparently he'd struck a nerve.

"Mercy Canyon is our home," Meg said. "We have friends here, people who love us. Who stood by us when we needed them."

Hugh thought of Sam's blustering kindness. "Friends are precious. I lost my closest buddy in that boating accident, and I'd give anything to have him back. I'm not suggesting that you give up your friends, Meg."

"It sure sounded like it."

"People move around a lot these days. You can keep in touch even if you don't stay in Mercy Canyon."

"You don't know what it's like to grow up the way I did." Her expression tense, Meg collected the mugs and took them to the sink. "Tim and I couldn't rely on our parents. Some nights we weren't even sure we would have a roof over our heads. If we hadn't had friends to rely on, I shudder to think what might have happened to us.''

"You're not a child anymore," Hugh pointed out gently. "And I would never let my daughter suffer like that."

"She needs security. Money is only part of it," Meg said. "She needs to know where she belongs, and so do I."

How could she shut out the larger world? "You can belong anywhere you want to."

"There's no point in discussing it." Meg finished washing the mugs and arranged them in the drainer. "I've got to get ready for work and take Dana next door to the sitter. Let me know when you get the test results, all right?"

"Certainly." Hugh supposed he'd rushed the matter of how Dana should be raised. Meg needed time to adjust to the situation.

Still, if Dana did turn out to be his daughter, they were going to make some changes. Later or, very possibly, sooner.

A HOUSE in the development where Sam and Judy lived, a fixer-upper with a garage workshop. That had been Meg's dream, and Joe's, too.

Why did Hugh have to talk about moving away from Mercy Canyon? And what was wrong with riding a scooter in the street? All the kids did it.

She drove to the restaurant with her thoughts a million miles away. Or a hundred miles, in West Los Angeles, which was practically the same thing.

Dr. Hugh Menton had wealth, power and prestige, none of which Meg craved. What she wanted for her daughter were the love and stability she'd lacked as a child.

Why couldn't Hugh be her Joe, content to stay in Mercy Canyon? He looked and talked like him, yet he was fundamentally different. Joe had been a fascinating mixture of boyish wonder and masculine confidence, with a hint of intellectual depth. In Hugh, the proportions were reversed.

He seemed mostly intellect with a strong sense of personal power. The boyishness only showed in tiny, precious glints.

She tried to imagine running her hands across those broad shoulders and unbuttoning his shirt. Perhaps removing that white coat he'd been wearing the other day. What would it be like, making love to Dr. Hugh Menton?

She ached to hold him in her arms. Her husband. She had no doubt Hugh was him.

He had to see that he belonged here, with Meg and Dana, that he couldn't rip them from their roots. He had to become her Joe again.

What if he couldn't? Maybe, if Meg didn't do as he wished, he would try to take Dana away.

Her chest squeezed so hard Meg could scarcely breathe. Surely he wouldn't be so cruel. Not the man she loved, even if he no longer loved her.

On the other hand, if his snobbish brother convinced him that it was for Dana's own good, who could tell what he might do?

Her distress must have been obvious when she got to work because, during a lull, Judy and Sam cornered her in the kitchen and demanded to know what had happened with Hugh. Meg told them about his suggestion that she move away from Mercy Canyon.

"He can't be Joe." Judy scowled. "Joe would never leave here. He loved this place."

Sam shook his head. "He's Joe. I recognize my buddy. He's just got his head screwed up from living the wrong way."

Miguel peered through the window from the front counter. "What do you mean, the wrong way? A doctor like that must make big bucks."

"Money isn't everything." Sam flipped a couple of burgers. "What he needs is for someone to set him straight."

Meg could feel her Irish temper rising. "You think I didn't try?"

"Nobody's picking on you, honey." Judy shot her husband a warning glance.

"He needs to come back here for a while." Judging by the gleam in Sam's eye, he was about to seize on an idea with his usual bulldog tenacity. "To live here so he remembers what it's like."

"Oh, come on!" snorted his wife. "You think Dr. High-and-Mighty is going to work in a coffee shop?"

"He did it before," Meg reminded her. "He was pretty good once he got the hang of things."

She smiled, remembering the first time Joe had tried to balance a tray of dirty dishes while opening the kitchen door. Sheer panic had showed on his face until she hurried to the rescue.

"You should talk him into it," Sam told Meg. "Really." He slapped some hamburgers onto buns and added a generous side of fries to the plates.

"She'd have as much luck talking a sea bass into serving itself for dinner," muttered Judy, and went out to check on her customers.

"She's right," Meg told Sam before he could argue. "Let's just hope he's the wrong man."

She scooped up the hamburger meals and went out, still not sure whether she meant what she'd just said.

On Tuesday, the DNA test came back positive.

From the expression on Andrew's face, Hugh thought at first that a patient had died or something else terrible had happened. Then his brother held out the fax.

Hugh read the results. The likelihood of such a match occurring by chance ranked in the tens of millions.

"I guess we know now where you spent that missing year and half." Andrew removed his stethoscope wearily. "Your first call should be to a lawyer."

Hugh sat down in his office chair and gestured his brother into a seat. The room was small and crammed with reference books.

Images and fragments of conversations collided in his brain. The sleepy town of Mercy Canyon. Children playing in the mobile home park. Sam gesturing as he worked in the restaurant kitchen.

Most of all, Meg and Dana Avery. His wife. His child.

"You're right," he said. "I need to find out if the marriage is legal."

Andrew shook his head. "No. I already checked. Even so, you'll need legal help to sort out the ramifications. Especially since there's a child."

Hugh didn't want to bring in a lawyer. "This is between Meg and me."

"Are you kidding?" Restlessly, Andrew sprang from his seat and began pacing. "She'll take you for every cent you've got. She might even get her hands on part of this practice. Had you thought of that?''

"She isn't after money." Hugh felt certain of that.

"You're so naive!" Andrew growled. "For heaven's sake, Hugh, don't fall into this woman's trap."

On the point of arguing, Hugh realized what lay behind his brother's antagonism.

While he was away, Andrew had been sued for malpractice when a patient, a young girl, suffered permanent knee damage after a car crash. The parents contended that he hadn't recognized the severity of her injury and should have referred her to a specialist immediately.

After several months of ugly accusations, some of which reached the press, it turned out that the couple had a history of suing people. Furthermore, the girl's minor injury had been exacerbated long after the accident when her father knocked her down in a fit of anger.

Although the suit was dropped and his reputation restored, Andrew had wasted a lot of time, money and anxiety. Perhaps some of his anger was finding an inappropriate target in Meg.

"No one's trying to trap me," Hugh said. "I know that whatever I decide will affect all of us, though. We need to call a family council."

They hadn't sat down to confer formally, the two of them along with their mother and Andrew's wife, since the death of their father seven years earlier. That was when Hugh and Andrew had decided to take over his practice jointly.

Andrew shrugged. "Why not? I'm sure Cindi and Mother will agree that you need to negotiate a settlement before this woman tries you in the press. Can you imagine what a story this would make?''

Hugh didn't like to think about it. He hoped he wasn't wrong about Meg because, if he was, she could make his life miserable.

Still, he didn't regret the DNA result. If Dana hadn't been his, the loss would have left a big hole in his life.

He wanted her. And, despite the differences in their attitudes, he wanted her mother, too.

THAT NIGHT, Meg dreamed about Joe for the first time in months.

They were on their honeymoon in the village of Laguna Beach. In a sunny hotel room, lulled by the murmur of the ocean beyond their window, they lay naked in bed.

Although she'd seen plenty of masculine bodies at the pool, none had been like Joe's. His wide shoulders tapered to a narrow waist and slim hips. Muscles and a flat stomach testified to his natural athleticism, but there was nothing of the show-off about him. No bulging biceps, no tattoos.

He slid one arm beneath her and rolled her toward him. Taking his time. Drinking in her soft contours, stroking and awakening her.

Meg had both longed for and feared this first moment of coupling with a man. Now a fierce joy sprang to life.

She wanted to take her husband inside her. Wanted to be one with him.

In the dream, she arched against him and only then noticed that he wasn't completely unclothed. A crisp white coat fell around his nude body, shielding them from the cool air.

As his mouth closed over hers, she reached eagerly for his hips. They were on the point of joining when she woke up.

Meg lay in bed, disoriented. Outside, a car muttered by, its headlights sweeping the far wall of the bedroom. A glance at the clock showed that it was after midnight.

Her body hummed with arousal. In the dream, it had been Hugh in bed with her, not Joe.

She hadn't wanted any other man since her husband disappeared. Did this mean Hugh was him, for sure?

Tomorrow, Wednesday, she would call to see if the DNA results had come back. Whatever the test said, Meg's heart knew the truth. She was defenseless against this man.

It seemed impossible that he could love her. And impossible that she could ever give him up.

Chapter Six

"I have a granddaughter?" Grace Menton stared at her younger son across the breakfast table.

Hugh wished he'd confided in his mother earlier, but he hadn't seen any point until they received the DNA results and knew for sure. "She's two years old and her name is Dana."

"This is bizarre." Cindi Menton poked her fork into a piece of melon. Hugh's tall, dark-haired sister-in-law wore a worried frown. "I mean, it's strange for them to turn up now, two years later."

"They weren't looking for a doctor named Hugh Menton. They were looking for a restaurant worker named Joe Avery." Hugh went on, detailing what he knew about his sojourn in Mercy Canyon and Meg's search for him.

Neither he nor Andrew would have chosen to hold a family council over breakfast, but last night Cindi hadn't returned from a PTA meeting until Grace was in bed. It seemed likely Meg would call today for the test results, so they needed to hurry their discussion. Andrew and Cindi's son and daughter, ages thirteen and eleven, had headed off to school and the housekeeper, Hannah, was busy in the kitchen. Alone at last, the four of them sat around the Victorian-style table, finishing their coffee and weighing the future.

As he talked, Hugh wondered what Meg would think of the flower-filled garden visible through the French doors and, beyond it, the pool sparkling in the autumn sunshine. Tucked into one corner of the property sat a play yard complete with a sandbox and swing set. Dana would love it, he thought.

"Hugh should sue for custody immediately, don't you agree?" At Andrew's comment, Hugh dragged his thoughts back to the present.

"Who would take care of the little girl while he's at work?" Cindi asked. "I'm always driving William and Angela to activities, and you know I'm president of the PTA this year."

"No one expects you to become Dana's baby-sitter," Hugh assured her.

"I'd like to know my littlest granddaughter," Grace said. "But I'm too old to be a mother again. I'm afraid I haven't the heart for it."

At sixty-two, Hugh's mother had weathered the death of her husband and Hugh's disappearance. Six months ago, when her beloved younger sister Meredith died of cancer, however, it became one blow too many. Although Grace continued to sponsor charitable events, she'd lost much of her zest for life.

Hugh reached out to touch his mother's hand. Giving him a startled look, she drew away.

How could he have forgotten that in the Menton clan, people kept a tight rein on their emotions? Maybe it was because, as Joe Avery, he'd learned how to share himself with others, Hugh thought.

"We could hire a nanny," Andrew said. "The point is, if Mrs. Avery keeps her daughter, she'll insist on child support. Her lawyer will demand every penny he can squeeze out of us.''

"That isn't a good enough reason to take a child away from her mother,'' Hugh said. "Besides, you're forgetting that Meg and I are married."

"It isn't valid,'' said Andrew.

"To be on the safe side, you should have it annulled,'' cautioned Cindi.

"That wouldn't erase my obligation,'' Hugh said. "Meg married me in good faith.''

"You don't know that.'' His brother rattled his empty coffee cup against the saucer for emphasis. "You don't recall what happened."

Hugh hadn't mentioned his visit to Mercy Canyon on Saturday and decided it would only annoy the others to bring it up now. Mentons were supposed to keep their private business to themselves, not go running around strange towns digging up the past.

Grace smoothed down a wing of silver hair. "I do think Hugh has a point, Andrew. There's no sense in antagonizing the young woman unnecessarily. She has a reasonable claim.''

"What are you suggesting?'' Her older son glared at a silver coffeepot on the sideboard as if it ought to fly to him of its own accord. Noticing her husband's focal point, Cindi got up and refilled his cup.

"She should come here and stay with us. Temporarily, of course,'' Grace said. "That way we can get to know each other.''

Meg, here? Hugh thought. Maybe she'd like it, especially when she saw what an ideal environment it was for Dana.

"I'll invite her,'' he said. "The first weekend she has free.''

"Should I plan a get-acquainted tea for her?" asked Cindi.

"Oh, please!" Andrew said. "Honey, it's kind of you to offer, but this young woman comes from a very different background. She's a waitress, for Pete's sake. What's she going to say to your society friends?"

"They're not snobs!" returned his wife.

"No one said they were," Grace replied smoothly. "However, if Meg accepts our invitation, we don't want to overwhelm her. Just getting to know the Menton tribe, with all our foibles, will be trying enough."

His mother's attitude impressed Hugh. "You should have been a diplomat, Mom."

"I might have been a lot of things." She sighed. "It's too late now."

"Being a Mom is the most important job in the world." Cindi smiled at her mother-in-law.

"I know that, dear, but thank you for reminding me," Grace said. "I'm just indulging in a bit of self-pity. In any case, do tell Meg that I'm eager to meet her, Hugh."

"I will," he promised.

ON WEDNESDAY MORNING, Meg found excuse after excuse to delay calling Hugh.

It was too early and the results wouldn't be in yet. He was probably busy with patients. She only had another hour to finish folding the laundry and get ready for work....

Maybe she shouldn't call at all, she mused as she folded laundry in the living room. Hugh frightened her. Not in any physical sense, but emotionally.

If she bonded with him again and then lost him, she would be devastated.

She wanted her Joe so much. Ached to be held in his arms, longed for the casual intimacies of eating and working and playing together. Yearned to see him light up when he heard Dana's chatter.

She'd seen the same need in her daughter. Dana had never shouted "Daddy!" at anyone else, not even Tim or Grandpa Zack, whom she'd known all her life. Was it fair to encourage her to love a man who might regret having fathered her?

Besides, no matter what the DNA test showed, Hugh Menton wasn't Joe. He had a whole range of experiences that Meg knew nothing about. The cozy world she'd built with her husband would never be the same with this stranger.

Unless Sam was right. Unless she could reawaken the part of Hugh that had been happy here in Mercy Canyon.

"Knock, knock." Her brother's face peered through the screen door. At twenty-three, Tim O'Flaherty retained some of his adolescent gangliness and most of the freckles that went with his red hair.

"You're back early." He'd driven his truck to Sacramento and wasn't expected to return until tonight. Tim rented a small apartment on the other side of town, but frequently ate with Meg when he was between girlfriends, like now.

"How could I stay away? I wanted to hear the latest installment in my sister's soap opera." Grinning, her brother let himself in and swooped up Dana as she ran to him. "How's my favorite niece?"

"Good!" said Dana.

"Did they get the results back?" Tim asked over his shoulder.

"I haven't called yet." Meg knew that was what he'd come to find out.

"Do it before you lose your nerve." Toting his niece on one hip, Tim prowled into the kitchen and opened the refrigerator. "I hope you got some more cheese. You were out last time."

Meg piled her clean laundry in the basket. "Yes. I got English muffins, too." Having helped raise her brother during their mother's final illness, she occupied a role somewhere between sister and aunt.

"I feel responsible for this whole business since I'm the one who spotted the newspaper photo." Tim returned, holding a package of string cheese in his free hand. "You want me to call him?"

"You wouldn't dare!" Meg said.

"Sure, I would," he replied cheekily. "Where's the phone number?"

"I'll do it." Grabbing the phone, she punched in the number.

Tim stuck his ear next to hers. "One ringy dingy. Two…"

"Hush!" A second later, the receptionist answered. Meg identified herself and asked for Hugh.

"I'll see if he's available," the woman said.

Tim made a face. As soon as they were on hold, he mimicked in a high voice, "I'll see if his lordship is available."

"The receptionist is very nice," Meg scolded. "And Hugh doesn't act like a…"

"Meg?" Hugh's warm voice vibrated over the line. "I'm sorry, I meant to call you, but the time got away from me."

"Sure it did," mouthed Tim.

"Ssh!" Into the phone, Meg said, "I'm sorry. My brother's here and he's acting immature."

"The one who noticed my picture?" Hugh said. "Hi, Tim."

"Hi," Tim said with a trace of embarrassment. "How's it going?"

"Fine. Could I speak to your sister alone, please?"

"Sure." His mouth twisting wryly, Tim retreated with Dana.

In the pause that followed, Meg realized she was about to receive the most important news of her life. Her hands went cold. "Did you get…?"

"It's positive," Hugh said. "You were right. I'm Joe." His tone revealed neither pleasure nor dismay.

Meg's heart hammered in her chest. She didn't know how she felt about the news.

Vindicated, of course. Even Andrew could see that she hadn't been lying.

Yet it was hard to reconcile the image of blue-collar Joe Avery with this doctor in a white coat. On his computer at home, Miguel had learned that Hugh Menton came from a distinguished family, was affiliated with a major hospital and, along with his brother, treated the children of movie stars and other notables.

Hugh was also the man, the DNA test confirmed, who had married Meg. Who had slipped off her bra and panties and made passionate love to her as ocean waves crashed in the background. The man who'd promised to love her forever and then disappeared.

"Where do we go from here?" she asked.

"I'd like for you and Dana to spend a weekend with my family as soon as you can spare the time," Hugh said. "I want you to get to know us."

The polite offer wasn't what she'd hoped for. He

hadn't said he was thrilled to be Dana's father. Or that he wanted to recapture the love they'd had.

"I...I can't," she blurted.

"Why not?"

"I wouldn't fit in." Although it might sound childish, she knew it was true.

"You don't have to fit in," Hugh said. "Just be yourself. The girl I married."

"Your brother said we aren't really husband and wife."

"Legally, we may not be," he agreed. "But Meg, we had a child together. There's a bond between us, like it or not."

"That doesn't sound very encouraging."

"I didn't mean it that way." His ruefulness reverberated over the phone. "This is a weird situation. Nobody was prepared for it. We have to find our own way."

"Our own way to what?" Although Meg didn't like pressuring him, compared to this important man and his upper-crust relations, she was at a disadvantage. Spending a weekend at his home would be like stepping unarmed into a lion's den.

"We have to decide how to raise Dana, how to make sure she gets the benefit of having two parents," Hugh said. "That's not all. Meg, I'm thirty-five years old and I was never tempted to get married before or since I knew you. There has to be something special between us."

"So I win by default?" she asked.

"Don't undervalue yourself," Hugh said. "You're pretty special."

She wanted more. She wanted to hear that he loved her, but she was kidding herself, Meg thought. In fact, she needed to be careful in case this invitation was the first step in an attempt to take Dana away from her. "I'll have to think about it," she said.

"There's no rush." In the background, she heard a woman tell Hugh a patient was waiting. "I have to go. Why don't you give me a call in a day or so? Here's my cell phone number."

She copied it down. "I'll get back to you."

"Take care. Give my love to our daughter." He hung up.

Our daughter. Meg shivered. Was that love or possessiveness?

Tim loped into the room, carrying the remnants of the cheese. "Dana's watching a tape. Well?"

"It's a go. He's Dana's father." Her knees suddenly weak, Meg sank onto the sagging couch. A spring dug at her hip.

"Why aren't you jumping for joy?" her brother asked. "You've found Joe and not only isn't he in jail, he's rich."

"You don't really think that's enough!" Meg hoped she'd taught her brother better values than that.

"It would help if he were generous, too," Tim admitted, plopping onto a chair.

"Tim! That isn't the right attitude."

"So what did he say?"

"He invited Dana and me to spend a weekend with his family," Meg said. "I wonder if he's going to seek custody of her."

"Maybe he's going to seek custody of you," said her brother.

"What do you mean?"

"It was obvious how much Joe adored you." He regarded her with knowing gray eyes. "A guy doesn't stop loving a woman just like that.'' He snapped his fingers.

''Try doing that''—she snapped hers in response—''for two years and see what it gets you.''

''Calluses,'' he replied.

In spite of herself, she giggled. ''You're outrageous.''

''What can it hurt?'' Tim leaned forward. ''Give the guy a chance. Let him spoil Dana, and you.''

Meg hugged herself protectively. ''What if I make a fool of myself in front of those society people?''

''How would you do that? You're not going to come down to dinner in your underwear!'' said her brother.

''I know, but...'' Keenly aware of her lack of education, Meg had compensated by learning to speak correctly and reading books about etiquette. To increase her cultural awareness, she'd attended local community theater productions and visited museums in San Diego.

However, she'd never been subjected to scrutiny. If the rest of Hugh's family was anything like Andrew, they would put her under a microscope.

''You're worried because you dropped out of high school, aren't you?'' Tim grew serious. ''You wouldn't have had to do that if Dad had acted like a father instead of a jerk.''

''Please don't blame him.'' Meg had forgiven their father, but Tim never had. ''That was a long time ago.''

''Look, sis, I'm glad you and Dad get along now and I know he's helped you since Joe disappeared,'' her brother said. ''That doesn't change the fact that he failed Mom for years and he wrecked my childhood. I have a right to be angry.''

''His birthday's in November,'' Meg said. ''His new lady friend is giving him a party this year and she asked me to invite you. She's an artist and I like her a lot, by the way.''

Zack had brought Lynn when he came down to escort Meg and Dana to the Fourth of July celebration in Oceanside. The two women had hit it off immediately.

''Don't count on me,'' Tim said. ''I wouldn't want to spoil the party by showing up and fighting with him.''

''Maybe you won't fight,'' Meg said. ''Just because you haven't spoken to him in years is no reason to avoid a situation that might turn out wonderful for everyone.''

''You should follow your own advice,'' Tim retorted. ''You won't go to Hugh Menton's house because people might sneer at you. They might like you, you know, and I don't see how they could not like Dana.''

On the brink of arguing, Meg remembered what Hugh had said. *There has to be something special between us.* Was he speaking theoretically or did he feel a stirring of his old attachment?

Maybe she ought to take the risk. Besides, she needed some leverage to get Hugh to spend time in Mercy Canyon as Sam had suggested.

''You're thinking a mile a minute, I can tell,'' said her brother. ''Have you changed your mind?''

''I'll go,'' Meg said. ''But only if Hugh agrees to come and spend a weekend in Mercy Canyon afterward.''

''Good idea. If there's time, I'd like to see if he can still beat me at swimming laps the way Joe used to,'' Tim said, his usual cheerfulness returning.

''He should. I'll bet he has his own private pool.'' Meg decided not to return to the subject of her father.

She and her brother had reached an impasse, for now. "I've got to hurry or I'll be late to work."

"I'll take Dana to the sitter." Tim uncoiled from the chair. "One more thing, sis."

"What?"

"Before you go to Rich Man's Land, do something about your hair," he said.

"What's wrong with it?"

"Everything."

Rosa had offered to cut her hair. Reluctantly, Meg conceded that it might be time to take her up on it. "I'll think about it."

HUGH WAS SURPRISED at how nervous he got as their scheduled weekend approached. He was glad Meg had agreed to his proposal, and didn't mind that she'd insisted on a reciprocal visit the following weekend.

He wanted to spend more time in Mercy Canyon. It was important to recover as many memories as possible, or they might be lost forever.

On the Friday that Meg was to arrive, Hugh felt off balance. He forgot about a medical society breakfast meeting and ordered an egg salad sandwich for lunch, even though he hated egg salad. He even ran out of the mints he usually kept in his pocket.

By arrangement, he left work sooner than usual. Meg had planned to drive up early to avoid rush hour traffic, and he wanted to be home when she arrived.

When he got there, however, her battered sedan waited in the curved driveway, its trunk roped shut. Again, a flicker of recognition and unease ran through Hugh.

A rough-looking man in the passenger seat, someone sitting behind him...

He couldn't summon any more. Maybe he didn't want to.

After parking on the side, Hugh entered the house through the back door. A hallway opened into the large kitchen, and there he glimpsed Meg standing at the counter, helping the housekeeper peel potatoes while Dana played with plastic bowls on the floor.

Before Meg spotted him, Hugh paused to drink her in. There was something different about her today. His family often chided him about being unobservant, and perhaps that was why it took a minute to realize she'd cut her hair.

Reddish-brown curls haloed her face, giving her an angelic air. She'd dressed differently, too. Beneath her apron, she wore tailored slacks and a trim short-sleeved sweater.

She looked sweet and lovely. It pleased Hugh that she'd gone to an effort to look nice for him.

More than nice. The sweater clung to her figure and the slacks outlined the flare of her hips. It was hard not to stride across the tile floor and pull her against him.

"You don't have to help cook dinner," he told her from the doorway. "Although I'm sure Hannah appreciates it."

The plump, gray-haired housekeeper, who'd worked for the family since Hugh was a teenager, nodded in agreement. "My arthritis bothers me. It's nice to have help."

"Let me do some, too." It hadn't occurred to Hugh that Hannah was getting old. "We should hire you an assistant. I'll speak to mother about that."

"It's not necessary," the housekeeper said. Her weary smile told him otherwise.

"If somebody will show me what to do, I'll get at it."

"You'll cut your fingers," Hannah warned. "You've never used a peeler."

"Yes, he has," Meg said. "Mostly we get the potatoes precut at the restaurant, but Sam has a few specialties he makes from scratch. You used to peel potatoes a couple of times a week, Joe. I mean, Hugh."

"I did?" Replacing Hannah at the counter, he picked up the small instrument. "It can't be much harder than stitching up a wound, right?"

"You may need to do that, too," the housekeeper warned. "Those instruments are sharp."

"Great kitchen you've got here," Meg went on. "Sam would love it."

"My mother says she bought the house for it," Hugh agreed. "Our joke is that she never stepped into it again."

The huge room featured two double sets of stainless steel sinks, a large center island with a counter and grill, three ovens, two dishwashers, an industrial-size refrigerator, two microwave ovens and endless cabinets.

It was what his mother called a catering kitchen, and that's the way she treated it, as if it were reserved for use by professionals. Grace did occasionally prepare a light lunch for herself, but that was the extent of her culinary endeavors. On Hannah's days off, Cindi cooked or ordered take-out.

To his surprise, the potato peeler fitted comfortably into his hand. After only a moment's hesitation, Hugh began stripping away the potato skin in an easy rhythm.

Hannah stared at him. "You do know how!"

"It's as if my hands know what to do even though my brain doesn't," Hugh admitted.

At his feet, Dana tired of the bowls and climbed to her feet. "Daddy hold me!" she said.

He set down the peeler and scooped up his daughter. It was the first time that he'd held her since he learned she was truly his, he realized. "You sure are a big girl."

She hugged him. "You big, too."

"Want something to eat?" he asked her.

Hannah looked indignant. "I fed her when she got here. I wouldn't let that child go hungry."

"You've been here awhile, then?" Hugh asked Dana.

"Half an hour." She rinsed the last potato. "Anything else I can do?"

"Let Hugh give you a tour before everyone gets home," Hannah said. "Go on, now."

"My pleasure," he said, and escorted Meg out of the kitchen.

He was glad to have her alone. Today, the distance between them seemed unnatural. Now that he knew she was his wife, he was eager to begin making up for lost time.

Chapter Seven

Hugh was looking at her differently today, Meg thought. More possessively. More intimately.

Were details of their life together coming back to him? It was startling to think that a man who was practically a stranger could be privy to her husband's intimate knowledge. On the other hand, she knew a great deal about this important doctor, too.

She knew how he chuckled deep in his throat when they were laughing together in bed. That he sometimes sang lullabies off-key, and winced at hearing his own mistakes. That he delighted in eating pancakes with peanut butter, a culinary treat to which Tim had introduced him.

Now, standing close to him in the hallway, she couldn't help being aware of Hugh as a man. His well-knit frame, boyishly springy blond hair and deep green eyes had mesmerized her from the first moment she saw him, dazedly stumbling from the passenger seat of Sam's van.

When she went to help, he'd gripped her shoulder and shot her a lost, pleading expression. His vulnerability had won her instantly.

She'd gone to Sam and Judy's house every day that

week until Joe regained his strength, and then mentored him at work. What a lost puppy he'd been—and what a completely adult, sensual male, she'd discovered the first time he took her in his arms.

"The housekeeper's apartment is through there. Hannah and her husband Marek, our groundskeeper, live there." Balancing Dana in his arms, Hugh pointed the way.

He mentioned, but didn't bother to show, the laundry facilities, although he did give her a glimpse into his mother's and Cindi's sprawling home office. That was where, Meg gathered, they kept track of their charitable and community activities.

Although she'd seen the front entryway and glimpsed the living room when she arrived, Meg was impressed all over again as they walked through. The space was nearly as large as a hotel lobby but much more beautiful, she thought, admiring the flow of muted pink, lavender, beige and turquoise in the carpets and draperies.

The dining room seated twelve, and the breakfast room could easily accommodate eight. At the back of the house, a den offered a big screen TV and the latest in sound equipment. Sam and Tim would love to watch football here.

"I'm disappointed," she said.

"You are?" Hugh tilted his head, suspecting a joke.

"Yes. Where's the gym?" Meg teased. "I can't believe you don't have one."

He grinned. "It's in the pool house, behind those trees." Through the long windows, she gazed across the broad lawn to where a stand of ficus shaded the pool.

"That's a relief," Meg said. "I thought maybe you were deprived."

"It is a bit much, I suppose." Hugh ducked his head. "I grew up here, so I take it for granted."

Dana, who'd been silent so far, perked up as she stared outside. "Go swim?" she asked hopefully.

"I hope you brought your suits," Hugh said.

Meg nodded. She'd bought a new one, along with a few other outfits, at Rosa's suggestion. "We can go later. I don't want my hair messed up when I meet your family.

"Speaking of your hair, I like it." He reached over and fluffed the curls.

Meg's blood shimmered as a silvery sensation coursed through her. She wondered if the contact had the same effect on Hugh and, if so, what he intended to do about it.

"Ready to head upstairs?" he asked.

"What?" She hadn't expected so bold a suggestion, not at this point.

"To see the other rooms," he said. "What did you think I meant?"

She ignored the question. "I saw our room when Marek carried up my suitcase. I brought a portable playpen for Dana to sleep in and he helped me set it up."

Realizing she was chattering out of nervousness, Meg fell silent. They stood there in the family room with late-afternoon sunshine flooding around them, just looking at each other.

He was so handsome, she thought. The familiar scar on his temple and the new one on his forehead only added to the rugged strength of his face. His green eyes were as mesmerizing as ever.

Hugh reached out and traced her cheek with his fore-
finger. He leaned down as if to kiss her, and Meg
moved closer instinctively. Waiting. Hoping…

Several rooms away a woman's voice called, ''I'm
home! Sorry to miss our guest's arrival. Where are you,
Hugh?''

They drew apart. The voice must belong to his
mother, Meg thought.

During their marriage, Joe had believed himself to
be an orphan. There'd been no in-laws to approve, or
disapprove, of Meg.

Now she prepared herself to meet the other most
important woman in her husband's life.

NOW THAT he was growing attuned to Meg again,
Hugh couldn't understand how he had lived for two
years without her.

He supposed he had dreamed of her. He recalled
awakening with vague impressions of a merry woman,
a sense of playfulness and his own rising physical desire. He'd dismissed the images as fantasies but they'd
been memories, and predictions of the future, too. Meg
belonged here, with him. He hoped his mother, a
woman of strong likes and dislikes, would approve.
Even if she didn't, Hugh intended to stand by his wife.

Grace Hancock Menton strode into the den. Tall and
self-possessed, she swept the room with a knowing
gray-green gaze that immediately targeted Meg.

He heard a slight indrawn breath beside him. If Meg
was intimidated, however, she gave no other sign of it.

''Welcome to our home,'' Grace said in her throaty
voice.

Meg shifted position, and for a moment Hugh feared
she might drop into an old-fashioned curtsy. Instead,

she reached to shake hands with her hostess. "It's my pleasure. Thanks for having us."

Grace turned toward the child in Hugh's arms. "And this must be…"

She stopped and stared at Dana. Hugh had never seen his mother at such a loss before.

Dana, delighted at the attention, clapped her hands to her cheeks and formed an *O* with her mouth. Then she giggled.

"I don't believe it!" Grace said. "Hugh, you've seen Meredith's baby pictures, haven't you? They look exactly alike!"

"Meredith?" Meg asked.

"My aunt," Hugh explained. "She died six months ago."

"I'm so sorry."

"Just look at her!" For once, Grace was too wrapped up to grow sad at the mention of her beloved sister. "I've missed her so much and this little doll looks exactly like her."

Much as he appreciated his mother's positive response, Hugh wondered if she was deluding herself. "What about the hair? Meredith was a brunette."

"She had much lighter hair when she was young. More brown than red, I guess, but it was curly and she had those same green eyes." Grace held out her arms. "Do let me hold her!"

Hugh transferred his daughter into her grandmother's clasp. Dana, cheerful soul that she was, busied herself toying with Grace's dangle earring.

"Don't pull on that," Grace warned in a light voice. "It would be a big owie for Grandma."

"Gra'ma?" Dana echoed brightly.

"Do you give this kid charm lessons or what?" Hugh asked Meg.

He was startled to see her eyes fill with tears. "My mother died when I was seventeen. Dana's never had a grandmother before."

Grace's gaze met Meg's, and in that moment Hugh could see a bond forming. *They need each other, and Dana needs them both.*

"I never thought when I lost my son that I would gain so much in the long run," his mother said.

"Has anyone mentioned that Dana has two cousins?" Hugh asked. "Angela's in sixth grade and William's in eighth."

"That's wonderful," Meg said. "I hope they don't mind a newcomer."

"I've told them all about her." Grace toured the toddler around the room, letting her pat a satiny couch cushion and pick up a CD to examine it. "William's not terribly interested, being a boy, but Angela loves having a baby in the family."

"So does Grandma," Hugh murmured.

"So I do, indeed!" Grace settled onto the sofa with Dana on her lap. "Do you like horsey rides, little girl?"

"Giddeyap!" announced Dana, and perched happily on her grandmother's knee. "Ride 'em!"

From the other side of the kitchen came the slam of the back door and the echo of voices. Hugh identified his nephew, loudly proclaiming his need for an after-school snack, and his niece asking about the baby.

Cindi and her daughter entered the room at the same time. Both had long dark hair, although Cindi's was frosted and worn in a French twist while her daughter's flowed around her shoulders. Angela plopped beside her grandmother and began playing with Dana.

Cindi regarded Meg with a hint of uneasiness. "Hello," she said. "I'm Andrew's wife, Cynthia."

"Better known as Cindi," Hugh added.

Meg smiled. "I'm Margaret, better known as Meg."

The two women studied each other. Hugh waited for his sister-in-law to make some friendly comment, but she seemed to have exerted herself as far as she could, or would.

She had, he recalled, offered to introduce Meg to her friends, so he didn't think she intended any hostility. Still, it was hard to know what to make of her stand-offish manner. "You have two children?" Meg said.

"William and Angela. They keep me busy." Cindi fell silent again.

Couldn't she at least make some comment about the baby? Hugh wondered. Until now, his brother's wife hadn't expressed any antagonism toward the new-comer. He decided to interpret her silence as simple awkwardness.

Besides, his mother and Angela were chortling and cooing enough for ten people. Soon William came in and demanded his mother's help with his homework, and the momentary discomfort passed.

Hugh wondered whether Meg's feelings were hurt. She seemed to take everything calmly, although he knew it must be daunting to meet so many people at once.

He wished for the first time that he didn't live in a big house. How much more pleasant it would be if he had his own quiet home where the two of them, or rather, the three of them could be together.

Well, when Meg was ready to marry him again, he'd

be happy to buy a place not too far away. Then they could be an active part of his family while retaining their privacy.

MEG WENT to her room to change for dinner. Although she'd never changed clothes for dinner before in her life, it made a good excuse to escape.

Dana was getting overstimulated, so she put her into the playpen for a nap. The little girl dozed off immediately.

The guest room was large and sunny. Meg sat on the edge of the double bed facing the window and gazed down over the lawn.

She had a good view of the pool, the pool house and tennis courts. Beyond, a tall fence covered by bougainvillea separated the property from another equally grand estate.

How could people feel comfortable living in such splendor? Wasn't it awkward being waited on by servants?

She knew Judy and Rosa would joke that they'd love to live like a queen, but they wouldn't mean it. Like Meg, they were used to doing things for themselves. Running their own kitchens and their own lives.

As for Hugh, he was as appealing in this mansion as in her trailer, yet he seemed more of a stranger, too. Because he belonged in this alien environment, and Meg didn't.

Thank goodness he'd agreed to go back to Mercy Canyon. Sam was right. Spending time with his old friends would help him become more like the Joe she'd known, and less like the product of this patrician family.

His family. Meg struggled to sort out her impressions. His mother obviously doted on Dana, but Cindi was another story.

Had she unwittingly offended her sister-in-law? Or did the woman object to being related to a waitress?

Of course, they weren't actually related. Hugh hadn't said anything about wanting to marry her again. Maybe she was only here on sufferance so everyone could get to know Dana.

A tap at the door startled her. "Meg?" Instead of waiting for an answer, Hugh turned the knob and came in.

"Shh!" Turning, she indicated their sleeping daughter.

He beamed at the little form curled beneath a blanket. "Cute," he whispered. "She's made quite a hit with my family."

Meg hugged herself. "I'm not sure I have."

"It takes Cindi a while to warm up." Hugh crossed the room toward her.

She scooted over to make room for him on the bed. They both sat facing the window, so their voices wouldn't disturb Dana.

"I'm looking forward to having you visit me again," Meg said. "This house is beautiful, but my place is cozier."

"You're right about that." Hugh smiled.

"I'm glad you agree."

"In fact, I've been thinking about buying my own place," he said. "There are some less pretentious houses a few miles from here."

Once he bought a house, he wouldn't want to move. Unless he moved back to Mercy Canyon, he would always belong more to his family than to Meg.

Perhaps, she thought with a twist of fear, he would

never belong to her again. "Why do you want your own place?"

"Privacy, for one thing."

"You want to be alone?"

"Not entirely alone." He shifted closer. "I was thinking of you."

"Of me?" Meg's heart leaped into her throat.

"I don't want to jump the gun." He slipped one arm around her. "I haven't even made love to you yet."

"What?"

A grin eased her flare of alarm. "Relax. I'm not planning a predinner seduction."

It was her turn to tease. "Why not?"

One eyebrow lifted. "Good question."

"I didn't mean that!" Meg said.

"Are you sure?" As he nuzzled her cheek, she caught a whiff of the same aftershave lotion Joe had worn, mixed with a trace of antiseptic soap. The result was an electrifying combination of the dearly loved and the tantalizingly unknown.

Hugh wore a crisp white shirt open at the collar. Much as she liked her blue-collar Joe, Meg had to admit there was something sexy about a man in a white button-down shirt.

She toyed with the top button, and saw Hugh's eyelids drift down. Drawn to him, she brushed her lips across the pulse of his throat.

A groan arose from deep within the man. Catching her in his grasp, he lowered his mouth to hers.

The sweet demand of his tongue filled Meg with excitement. She looped her arms around his shoulders and gave herself over to his kiss.

Her hands found the firmness of his chest and

stroked down to his flat stomach. When Hugh lifted her onto his lap, she felt his hardness.

He smoothed her hair back from the temples and gazed at her mistily, then eased her against one arm. With his free hand, he caressed her breasts through the sweater until the pressure of his thumb on her nipples shot fire into Meg, threatening to melt her inhibitions.

Not here. Not now.

Reluctantly, she gripped his hand and halted the alluring motion. Hugh paused, his breathing ragged. "Do we have to stop?"

Meg didn't know how to answer. After saving herself all her life for her husband, she was startled to find herself responding with savage heat to this stranger.

Who was, and wasn't, Joe.

"I'm not ready," she said.

"I can't say the same for me." Reluctantly, Hugh helped her off his lap. "However, I consider that a promising start. I suppose I should let you get ready for dinner now, shouldn't I?" Humming softly, he rose and went out the door.

A promising start? Meg was tempted to throw a pillow at him, except that it might disturb Dana.

That man was delightfully infuriating. He always had been. How could she have forgotten?

HUGH STILL hadn't heard from the Whole Child Project, and his phone calls hadn't been returned. Hope was waning, much to his brother's satisfaction, but he wasn't ready to give up.

Two weeks remained before the project officially got under way. No doubt they'd had dozens of applications to consider and many interviews to schedule since his own in August.

On Saturday, he took Meg for a drive to check his mail at the office. "I'm expecting something important," he explained, knowing it was probably useless but unable to contain his impatience until Monday.

They left Dana in Grace's loving care. She and Angela doted on the child, forming a welcome relief from Cindi's continued silences and Andrew's stiffness.

Beside Hugh, Meg settled gingerly onto the plush seat of his sedan. She formed a splash of autumn color with her halo of auburn hair glowing above a russet sweater and brown slacks.

"You look great," he said.

"So do you." Her gaze lingered briefly on his short-sleeved sport shirt, open at the collar.

Hugh, feeling his heart rate accelerate, struggled to wrench his thoughts away. "Are you enjoying your visit so far?"

"For the most part, yes," Meg said as he navigated the curving streets of the Hollywood Hills. "I wish your brother liked me, though."

"It's nothing personal." He swerved around a double-parked delivery truck. "He's afraid I'll leave again."

"I suppose I must seem like a threat to him, don't I?" Meg said wistfully.

"No," Hugh replied firmly. "The truth is, I've changed since I got back. Wealthy people's children need good care like everyone else's, but I want to accomplish something more meaningful."

Her expression lightened. "Like working in a small town with ordinary kids?"

"Not exactly." She'd misinterpreted him, Hugh saw. "You see, I've applied..."

"I didn't mean Mercy Canyon necessarily," Meg

said quickly. "There are lots of other towns within commuting distance. Oh! I wasn't implying that you should move in with me or anything."

"It's all right." Hugh was pleased that she wanted to keep him close.

But he wasn't Joe. In that life, he gathered, he'd been willing to drift with the tide, perhaps because he'd literally washed ashore. A physician version of Joe would be happy to run a medical office in a small town.

Hugh Menton had a sharper edge. Like it or not, he possessed a driving ambition, perhaps inherited from his father, along with a social conscience that must have come from his mother.

Frederick Menton had been an immigrant French physician. His skills had so impressed his American mentor, the eminent pediatrician Benedict Hancock, that they'd formed a partnership. Later, Frederick married Benedict's daughter, Grace, and drove himself relentlessly in his work until he suffered a fatal heart attack at the age of seventy.

Unlike his father, Hugh felt no need to seek the high opinion of society. He needed to succeed in ways that were meaningful to him, however, and that meant reaching out to patients in a new way.

He still hadn't mentioned the project, Hugh saw, but the heavy traffic in West L.A. demanded all his attention. He would tell her later.

"Look at those crowds!" Meg eyed the pedestrians window-shopping at boutiques. "How can people feel comfortable living among so many strangers?"

"City dwellers form communities of their own. Like islands in an ocean," Hugh said.

"Islands are isolated," Meg pointed out. "I wouldn't like that."

"Some people consider small towns isolated."

She didn't answer. He hoped she didn't think he looked down on Mercy Canyon. Hugh liked the place; he just knew that, personally, he needed a wider scope.

They pulled into the parking garage beneath his office building. Beside his reserved space rested Andrew's car.

"I didn't know your brother was working." As they waited for the elevator, Meg sounded dubious about the prospect of seeing him, and Hugh didn't blame her. Andrew's manner had been somewhat brusque at dinner and breakfast.

"Couldn't you have asked him to check your mail?"

"He's not exactly enthusiastic..." The elevator arrived at the same time as a janitor, who rattled his cart inside and rode up with them. Hugh fell silent.

Upstairs, the receptionist, Chelsea, greeted Meg eagerly. The staff had been fascinated by the news that she was Hugh's long-lost wife. "It's great to see you again, Mrs. Menton."

"I'm not...well, thanks," Meg said. "It's good to see you, too."

There weren't many patients in the waiting room, since no regular checkups were scheduled on Saturdays. Hugh and Andrew alternated staffing the office for two hours on the weekend to help patients suffering from acute illnesses.

Helen appeared a few minutes later. "How's your little girl? Doing better?"

"Her ears are fine," Meg said. Hugh, who had brought his implements home for that purpose, had checked Dana yesterday and pronounced her recovered.

"My mother's crazy about her," he added.

"I'll bet!"

As they reached his private office, Andrew stopped by. He nodded to Meg and indicated the few pieces of mail on the desk. "It's not there. I already checked. It's time you quit kidding yourself, bro."

Hugh's stomach twisted. Over the past two years, he'd experienced a growing conviction that he'd regained his skills as a doctor for some higher purpose than to do routine work.

If this project had passed him by, he didn't know what that purpose was. And, Hugh realized suddenly, he couldn't resolve any of the other uncertainties in his life until he found out.

Including his future with Meg.

Chapter Eight

"What's not there?" Looking from brother to brother, Meg got the distinct impression that she'd been left out of the information loop.

"Hugh has delusions of being Albert Schweitzer," Andrew said.

"He's going to Africa?" she asked in dismay.

"No," Hugh said. "I've applied for a position with a research project in Orange County."

At least he wasn't going far away. Whatever this research position was, though, Meg knew it might affect her future, too.

"Thank goodness he isn't joining the Peace Corps." Andrew grimaced. "He's not quite as far gone as our dedicated cousin Barry."

"Aunt Meredith's son is a pediatrician, too," Hugh explained. "He's spent two years working on a remote island."

"I'm not sure the inner city is much better," Andrew said.

Meg turned to Hugh questioningly. "The research project would serve children in the poorer areas of central Orange County," he told her. "It doesn't look like

I'm going to get the job, unfortunately. I should have heard by now.''

''Where would you live if you do get it?'' she asked.

''Pacific West Coast University Medical Center is located in the city of Orange, in Orange County, so I'd want to live there,'' he said. The town was located between Mercy Canyon and Hollywood Hills, too far from either for a comfortable commute, Meg thought.

''There's not much future in it,'' Andrew warned. ''It's only a two year project and you'd be giving up a lucrative practice. You've got a daughter to support now.''

Hugh's jaw tightened. ''It pays a respectable salary, and if the grant gets renewed, it could last much longer.''

Meg didn't want him to take a job that far from Mercy Canyon. Still, she was heartened to learn that Hugh had been thinking of leaving his partnership. If the research position didn't come through, maybe he would rethink her suggestion of opening an office near her and Dana.

After saying goodbye to Andrew, they returned to the house, ate lunch and went swimming. Although disappointed over the lack of a letter, Hugh quickly regained his usual good spirits.

While Meg swam laps, he and Dana played in the shallow end. The two romped as if they'd spent the past two years being best buddies.

Sunlight danced across Hugh's sharply defined face. With his bold green eyes and sculpted sandy hair, he set Meg's pulse racing.

Beneath this sophisticated exterior beat the heart of the man she loved, and who loved her. What she needed to do was gradually, slowly, gently bring him back to his senses.

Climbing out of the pool, she stretched and felt his gaze run across her body. The dark blue swimsuit enlivened by a single, large lily design had appealed to her for its subtlety but, as the fabric clung to her breasts, she realized it wasn't as subtle as she'd thought.

If only they could go back to the house, put Dana down for a nap and retire together, to undress each other lovingly....

Someday they could have more children, Meg mused, sitting so her feet dangled in the water. A red-haired boy to toddle after his sister at the playground. Perhaps he or Dana would grow up to be a doctor like their father.

She blinked. When had Meg O'Flaherty, high-school dropout, dared to imagine her children becoming doctors?

Certainly she wanted them to pursue their dreams. But Meg knew where she belonged, and it wasn't in pretentious high society being snubbed by people like Cindi Menton. She was proud to be a small-town waitress.

Hugh would have to meet her on her own ground, and the sooner the better. As for their children, anything constructive they wanted to do would be all right with her.

"So," she said as father and daughter got out of the pool. "Are you coming to visit us soon?"

"Next weekend," he said. "I can't leave until after my morning office hours, but that'll give us a day and a half. I'd like to spend as much time as possible in Mercy Canyon."

"You would?" Hugging her knees, Meg waited hopefully for more.

"My memories started returning when I was there." Toweling off Dana's hair, Hugh grinned at its fuzzy wildness. "I recognized the coffee shop, and Sam and Judy."

"You still know how to peel potatoes," Meg pointed out. "Anything else come back to you?"

A mischievous look played across his face. "Nothing I can talk about in public."

Her skin tingled. Did he mean their lovemaking? If he recalled that, then maybe the old Joe would soon begin to reemerge.

Not exactly as he'd been, of course. She wasn't foolish enough to hope for that. Hugh was more polished and certainly better educated. What she needed was for him to belong in her world, where she felt safe.

"I'm glad," she said. "I want you to remember everything."

"It might make me dangerous," he teased.

"I'm looking forward to it."

THEY HAD LEFT their clothes in the large pool house, which, in addition to an exercise room, contained a guest bedroom. Hugh, who needed only a minute to change, used the bathroom first, then went into the kitchenette to fix a snack for Dana.

Meg, concerned about the chlorine's effect on her hair, decided to shower. "Is there a hair dryer?" she called.

"It's fully equipped. Angela and William have their friends over to swim all the time." Hugh remembered a key point. "By the way, I noticed the fan's broken.

You might want to leave the door ajar so the mirror doesn't steam up.''

"Okay." She grabbed her clothes on the way in.

From the refrigerator, Dana chose a carton of vanilla yogurt. "Ice cream!" she said.

"Almost." Hugh wondered if he should feed it to her, but she handled a spoon well, only dribbling a little onto the countertop.

Afterward, he settled her at William's video game station. Although Dana couldn't play well, she loved pressing the controller and watching the figures jump.

Hugh went to collect the wet swimsuit he'd left on the tile floor near the bathroom. As he scooped it up, he heard the water cut off and, without thinking, glanced into the steamy interior.

Meg emerged from the shower enclosure, absorbed in drying her legs. He glimpsed full, pink-tipped breasts and an alluring navel.

Embarrassed to be spying on her, he hurried away. He didn't think Meg had noticed his stolen glimpse.

It registered full-force on Hugh's masculine instincts. He grew almost painfully hard, and his skin flushed at a thousand points.

He hadn't been kidding about remembering her. And what he didn't recall, his imagination gleefully supplied. Her welcoming softness. The thrill of stroking inside her. The mounting tension…

"Daddy! TV!" Dana planted himself in front of him and pointed at the big screen.

"Sure, sweetheart." Moving a little stiffly, Hugh went to find the remote control.

ON SUNDAY, Meg had to leave in the early afternoon. Having missed two nights at the Back Door Cafe, she'd promised to return for today's second shift.

After packing, she went to give Hannah a hug. The housekeeper said goodbye with genuine regret.

"Hugh is a good man," she told Meg. "Yesterday, he asked his mother to hire me an assistant, and she's going to do it."

"I know he's a good man," she said. "I'm just not sure whether he's still *my* man."

"I've known him for twenty years," Hannah said. "He's had girlfriends, but no one like you. You're the right one."

"Thank you." Meg squeezed her one more time in parting.

This weekend, her view of Joe—of Hugh—had changed, she reflected. She'd come to accept that his family and people like Hannah had claims on him, too, and knew him in ways that Meg didn't.

She would have to share him. That was fine, as long as she got the main part, she decided with an inner smile.

Andrew had gone out golfing, to her relief, and Cindi was driving her children to a friend's house. Meg loaded the suitcase in her trunk and was about to go inside for the playpen when a shiny red sport utility vehicle veered up the driveway.

It halted abruptly. Cindi stared at Meg through the open window as if about to say something.

Something unpleasant? Now was the woman's chance, with no one else listening, Meg thought.

Might as well get it over with. She approached the SUV cautiously. "I'll be leaving in a few minutes."

"Did you—did you have a good time?"

That was an odd question from a woman who'd scarcely spoken to her all weekend except to answer direct questions. "Yes, I did."

A pause followed. Finally, Cindi said, "Your daughter's cute."

"Thanks. Your kids are terrific. Angela really made a hit with Dana."

"She loves playing with the baby." The dark-haired woman showed more animation than before. "Sometimes she's moody. It was good to see her loosen up."

"I guess adolescence is tough for kids and parents," Meg said. "When Dana gets there, I'll ask your advice."

"I'm not sure I'll know anything useful," Cindi said with a smile. "You were good for Grace, too. She took her sister's death hard."

"That's understandable."

"In Dana, she got a little of Meredith back," Cindi said. "I hope we'll see you again before long. Have a safe trip home."

"Thanks," Meg said.

The SUV took off around the side of the house, leaving her bemused. Why hadn't it occurred to her before that Cindi was simply shy? It must have taken her the whole weekend to feel comfortable with a newcomer.

A few minutes later, Meg was ready to leave. Dana, strapped into her car seat, waved out the window to Daddy and Grandma Grace.

"Bye-bye!" announced the toddler. "See ya!"

Meg wished she and Hugh could have a few private minutes. Next weekend, she vowed to make the most of their time together.

Still, it was wonderful to see the joy on Mrs. Menton's face. This grandmother would never be standoffish, Meg felt certain.

Hugh came around to her window. "I'll come as early as I can on Saturday," he promised.

"I have to work that evening." Meg couldn't leave her post two weekends in a row. "It'll give you more time with Dana, though."

"We'll find lots of ways to get into trouble, I'm sure." He hesitated, and for a minute she thought he was going to kiss her through the window.

Then he walked around the car, leaned in and kissed Dana instead. Meg supposed it was the discreet thing to do with his mother looking on, but she didn't want to be discreet.

She wanted to be Joe's nearest and dearest. She wanted to be his wife. Or, rather, Hugh's, Meg reminded herself.

"Goodbye." As she waved, Cindi came out of the house and joined the others.

"We'll miss you!" she called.

Life was full of surprises, Meg thought, and started the car.

THE ENVELOPE bearing the return address of Pacific West Coast University Medical Center arrived on Thursday.

Chelsea handed it to Hugh the moment he emerged from an examining room. "I wanted to be sure you got it first," the receptionist said with a wink. "You never know what Andrew will do, and it's so thick it would break the shredder."

Her hair, he noticed, had turned raven black since yesterday. It might be the latest fad, or perhaps Chelsea was setting a trend.

Neither of them really believed Andrew would destroy the letter. However, Hugh knew the staff was as eager, and perhaps as apprehensive, to learn the news as he was.

"Thanks." He carried it into his office, his heart pounding. It brought back his anxiety from the day he received his letter of acceptance to college, and then, four years later, to medical school.

What if the answer was no?

His hands felt clammy as he fumbled to open the envelope. The flap refused to separate, and he had to grope through his desk drawer for an opener to slit it.

He lifted out a thick sheaf of folded papers. One edge caught on the opening and he had to yank it out, ripping the envelope. Had the senders purposely made this letter as difficult as possible to read?

His hand felt unsteady as he unfolded the papers and read the top sheet out loud.

"Dear Dr. Menton, I am pleased and honored to welcome you...apologize for the delay...hope to have you onboard shortly...housing available near campus..." He scanned down to the signature.

"Vanessa Archikova, M.D. Director, Whole Child Project."

She, along with a panel of consultants, had interviewed him for several hours. They'd quizzed him, told jokes, eaten lunch in the university faculty center, and probed for his philosophy of medicine and his reasons for wanting to join the program.

They'd seemed fascinated by his bout of amnesia, although Hugh had feared that such a perceived weakness might put them off. Apparently it hadn't.

In a burst of triumph, he was tempted to throw back his head and shout. Only the fact that there were patients in the office restrained him.

Along with the letter, Dr. Archikova had sent an application for off-campus housing and other employment related forms, plus an invitation to a get-acquainted reception in two weeks. Hugh left them on his desk for later.

He hurried to check on his next patient, a baby arriving for a well-care visit. Then another, and another. The edge of his excitement was blunted, but only slightly, by the time the suite emptied for lunch.

Hugh finished jotting down notes about the last patient and looked up to see his brother, Chelsea and Helen waiting outside his office. Andrew's arms were folded. Helen's raised eyebrows urged him to speak, while Chelsea twisted her hands nervously.

"Yes," Hugh said. "I got it."

"Good for you!" Chelsea gave him the thumbs-up.

"Congratulations," said Helen.

Andrew glowered.

Neither of the women showed quite as much enthusiasm as Hugh had expected. It struck him that his departure would affect them as well as his brother.

"They'd like me to start in two weeks," he said. "I'm sorry to give such short notice."

"We can cover for a while," Andrew said. The office had a reciprocal arrangement with several other doctors' groups to help out when anyone was short-handed. "I'll need to bring in someone else as soon as possible, though. We've expanded since you got back, and I don't want to lose the momentum."

"Should I reschedule appointments?" Chelsea asked.

"Don't change anything yet," Andrew said.

In his face, Hugh read the rebuke that he was abandoning his responsibilities. Letting people down in a way their father wouldn't have approved.

If only he could help solve the problem he himself had created. Maybe he could.

"I've got an idea," Hugh said. "I might know someone for the job."

Skepticism darkened his brother's expression. "This ought to be interesting."

Hugh didn't want to say any more. As soon as the others left, however, he fired off an e-mail. Then, too excited to eat a sandwich at his desk, he went for a walk.

As his long swinging strides carried him past office towers and boutiques, Hugh's heart sang. He'd been hired. He was going to tackle a wonderful challenge, to use his medical skills in a pioneering project.

His stroll carried him past the Los Angeles Museum of Art, a mushrooming complex of galleries. On the same grounds, the La Brea Tar Pits gleamed treacherously, as serenely deceptive as in the days when mastodons and saber-toothed tigers had ventured into the watery shallows and been trapped forever.

Standing on the sidewalk outside the fenced tar pits, Hugh watched tourists photographing a mastodon statue that towered over the scene. When Dana got older, he mused, he would take her to the adjacent Page Museum to see the reconstructed skeletons of ancient animals.

Thinking of Dana reminded him that he ought to notify Meg about his good fortune. He was about to reach for his cell phone when he stopped.

Better to give her the news in person so they could discuss their next step. The fact that he was moving away from his family to a friendly college town should help reconcile her to leaving Mercy Canyon. They were going to get a fresh start. It was perfect timing, Hugh thought, and strolled toward a nearby cafe to eat lunch.

"I AGREE. The place would be perfect for a doctor's office," said Meg's next-door neighbor, Abbie Lincoln.

The sixty-four-year-old, who baby-sat Dana along with her own five grandchildren, stood studying the vacant storefront that Meg had pointed out to her. It was wedged between a coin laundry and a thrift store off Mercy Canyon's main road.

Formerly a dentist's office, the place ought to have the right hookups, or whatever a doctor needed, Meg thought with satisfaction. "I'm glad you like it."

Although Mercy Canyon's population was only about eight hundred, its businesses drew customers from the surrounding canyons. There were small farmers, some New Age types who lived in wilderness cabins, and the on-site workers from an inland hot springs retreat.

Surely a pediatrician could find plenty of patients here. Especially with free word-of-mouth advertising at the coffee shop.

The two women resumed their walk, pushing the battered strollers at an easy pace. As they traveled, Dana and Abbie's eighteen-month-old granddaughter Bev babbled at each other in a nonsensical dialogue.

"I was thinking about asking how much it rents for, but maybe that's too pushy," Meg said. "What do you think?"

"I'd leave that to your husband." Abbie had met Joe in the old days and still considered them married. She also took it for granted he would settle down with his family as before.

Meg felt a twinge of apprehension. Until she'd seen

the Menton estate, she hadn't fully grasped the differences between Hugh and Joe. Could he really feel comfortable here again?

They didn't have to live in her cramped mobile home, she reminded herself. They could buy a house, or at least a more spacious unit.

"That's enough exercise for one day." Abbie turned her stroller at the next corner and they headed back.

"Thanks for coming with me," Meg said. "I appreciate your opinion."

"Any time," her neighbor replied airily.

By the time they reached home, it was a quarter to eleven. Meg decided to join the crowd at the bowling alley.

Hugh wasn't likely to arrive before one o'clock. Just in case, though, she left a note on the door to tell him where she was going.

Chapter Nine

On Saturday morning, fishermen dotted the broad Oceanside Pier all the way to the restaurant on the end. Hugh stood by a railing, thinking about the man whose identity he had unwittingly assumed.

Yesterday, one of the last missing pieces in his puzzle had lodged in place when he called to check with the Oceanside police. The previously unidentified drowning victim had turned out to be Joe Avery of Tennessee, an officer said.

Hugh had called Joe's next of kin, a cousin to whom he'd spoken on the phone when he believed himself to be Joe, to express his condolences. He still didn't feel, though, that he'd adequately acknowledged the man whose life had intersected his in a unique way.

He'd expected to work this morning. However, Andrew had found a retired pediatrician who could fill in until a permanent replacement was arranged. The man had suggested that he come in today to become familiar with the office, and Andrew wanted to be there to supervise.

Since Meg wasn't expecting him until later, Hugh had detoured to this beach community to pay his last respects.

From this vantage point, he could see far across the water, bathed in late September sunshine. Through the diamond sparkles glided a couple of sailboats much like the one his friend Rick had owned.

Hugh's throat tightened. Three and a half years ago, on a day much like this one, he and Rick had decided to sail from Dana Point down to San Diego. Both had craved the relaxation after a hard week at their respective medical practices.

Even now, Hugh didn't understand how the large yacht had drawn so near without anyone on either craft noticing. The sun must have been in his and Rick's eyes, while the yacht's pilot, according to the Coast Guard report, had been drinking.

A sudden wash of water in the yacht's wake had flipped the sailboat like a pancake. Although they should have known better, neither doctor had worn a life jacket.

Exactly how Rick had sunk beneath the waves, Hugh didn't know. He would always regret that he hadn't somehow been able to save his friend.

He'd scarcely saved himself. According to Meg, he'd swallowed a lot of water and nearly drowned. If the lifeguards hadn't been out searching for Joe Avery, they might not have found Hugh Menton in time.

So, he realized, he had come here to say farewell to two men. And, in a way, to the part of himself that had been born that day and lived for eighteen months.

"I never really believed you were Joe," the cousin had said yesterday when Hugh called. "You were so intent on finding the truth, so focused. Joe wasn't like that. He was kind of a lost soul."

Hugh walked slowly along the pier, skirting the fishermen with their rods and buckets of bait. The scent of grilling hamburgers from the restaurant mingled with the fishy smell of the ocean.

A shadow moved with him, invisible but keenly felt. The spirit of Joe Avery.

Hugh wasn't sure whether he sensed the real man from Tennessee or his own alter ego. They blended into one in his mind, a single drifter in search of anchorage.

He had come here today to help Joe's spirit find peace, or perhaps to help himself integrate past and present. He knew now that it wouldn't happen all at once. It would take more time.

Near the end of the pier, Hugh stopped and held out a bouquet of white roses. "Goodbye, Joe," he said aloud, and dropped them.

His eye marked the path of the white buds as they plummeted down, down, down into the waves. From here, the water looked cold and dark, not shimmering as in the distance.

The flowers bobbed and bumped against the pilings, tangling in some seaweed. Gradually, the stems separated and vanished from view.

Joe's spirit remained, though. Hugh could feel the man restlessly seeking a place where he belonged. *He was kind of a lost soul.*

Thoughtfully, Hugh walked from the pier to the parking lot and got in his car. His invisible companion faded from his awareness until, by the time he hit the freeway, his thoughts turned to his remaining mystery.

He still didn't know what had happened the day he disappeared from the gas station. He couldn't even remember arriving there with Meg, let alone why or how he left.

Perhaps the information would come back this weekend. More importantly, he and Meg could begin making plans together now that he had landed his new job.

His mood lightened. He was alive and he had found the woman he loved. Silently, he thanked both Joe Averys.

When he arrived in Mercy Canyon, Hugh easily found the trailer park. He was about to rap on the door when he saw Meg's note.

Disappointed, he read that she'd gone bowling. Although he knew it meant only a brief delay before he saw her, he'd visualized himself walking into the trailer and swooping her off her feet while Dana danced around them.

Instead, he needed to meet her at the lanes. Well, part of the point of this weekend was to circulate among his old acquaintances, so why not enjoy the occasion?

Holding on to a positive mood, he drove to Mercy Lanes. In the sunshine, the strip mall dozed peacefully, but once Hugh stepped inside, he entered a world of noise and action.

The rumble of balls. The crash of pins. The ching-ching and mechanized shouts of video games.

After his eyes adjusted to the dim light, he made out a group of people lounging on a bench. Sam. Judy. Rosa. Ramon. With a start, Hugh registered the fact that he recognized the Hispanic couple, whom he hadn't seen on his last visit.

As he approached, heads turned and Sam waved. Meg, facing the pins with a ball in her hand, didn't see him.

She strode forward and released the ball in a smooth arc. It flew along the boards and shot pins into the air.

"Strike!" she shouted, and then she saw him. "Oh!

You're early!'' She ran toward him, her hair haloing her flushed face.

''Andrew took over for me.'' Self-conscious in front of the others, Hugh slipped one arm around her waist instead of hugging her. ''I'm glad you left the note. Where's Dana?''

''With my neighbor, Abbie,'' she said.

''We'll see her soon, though?''

''As soon as we get home.'' Meg swayed against him as they approached the others. Light perfume drifted up, bringing images of candlelight and soft sheets.

''It is him!'' Rosa announced.

''You dyed a purple streak in your hair,'' Hugh said. ''It's dramatic.''

''You like it?'' The beautician patted the colorful strand for emphasis.

''You remember what she looked like before?'' Sam said. ''You're coming along, my friend.''

''Yes, but does he remember how to bowl?'' Judy asked.

A scene came to Hugh. Himself, feeling all thumbs, lofting a ball and watching it plop into the gutter. ''How can I remember what I never knew?'' he said. ''I was a complete klutz.''

''I'm sorry to hear the good doctor isn't any better at this sport than Joe used to be,'' Ramon said. ''That's okay. Somebody has to be worse than I am.''

Amid good-spirited joshing, Hugh joined the crowd. Sure enough, he barely knocked over a couple of pins with his first ball and threw the second one into the gutter.

''You wouldn't want to spoil your record,'' Sam joked. ''Otherwise, we might not be sure it was you.''

At one o'clock, the Hartmans invited him and Meg to the cafe for lunch. Ramon and Rosa departed to their respective shops.

In the coffee shop, Miguel was holding down the fort, aided by a waitress and fill-in cook that Hugh didn't recognize. There was, he mused, a lot of turnover in the restaurant business.

"That new guy you hired to come in this afternoon just called," Miguel told Sam. "He broke his ankle, or so he says. And I've got to go meet my grandma at the airport. She's flying into San Diego from Phoenix."

"Don't even ask me to work late," said the waitress on duty. "My boyfriend's watching the kids till two, but then he has to report to his job."

"Meg, I need you to come in early." Sam's tone filled with pleading. "And Joe, I mean Hugh, is there any way you could fill in at the counter?"

Hugh's memory didn't extend to his assistant manager duties, he realized with a twinge of alarm. Still, how could he let his friend down?

"I'll do my best, if Meg doesn't mind," he said.

She folded her arms, mixed emotions fleeting across her face. With a sigh, she said, "I was looking forward to some private time, but I don't guess we have much choice. I'll call Abbie and see if she can keep Dana."

As it turned out, the neighbor was happy to take the little girl along with a couple of her grandchildren to visit a friend's farm. They would eat dinner there and come home late.

That left Hugh to help serve a bunch of customers who innocently assumed he knew what he was doing.

IN THE BACK, Meg retrieved her uniform, a gray skirt and blouse covered by a white apron, from a locker while Hugh changed into Miguel's spare outfit. She couldn't help chuckling at the idea of a physician serving dinner at a coffee shop.

"I'm glad to see the place is clean," Hugh commented when he emerged from the men's room. "Germs can easily breed in a place like this."

The gray shirt fit tightly across his muscular chest and the matching slacks emphasized his lean hips. Even in the low-key clothing, the confident squareness of his shoulders and tilt of his chin telegraphed the fact that he was a man of importance.

Or so it seemed to Meg.

"Sam and Judy take pride in their restaurant," she assured him. "So did you, when you worked here."

"Good." Hugh paused in the short hallway that led out to the public areas. "What are my duties?"

"You take orders at the counter," Meg said. "Make sure everything's running smoothly, field any complaints, keep the coffeepots and cups filled. Judy and I can handle the tables and the cash register."

"Thank goodness. I wouldn't know which key to press." He looked genuinely concerned.

"Lucky for you, you've got two experienced waitresses on duty," she said. "If anything goes seriously wrong, report it to Sam immediately."

"I'll do my best." Hugh gave her a boyish grin. "It's not as if he can fire me if I mess up, right?"

"He can chew you out good," she returned. "They'll hear him all the way to West L.A."

"That's a scary thought. Well, here goes nothing." After giving her a quick kiss on the cheek, he passed down the hall and into the line of fire.

What a good sport, Meg thought. Most men would have grumbled about the inconvenience.

That was her Joe. He fit in easily wherever he went. Once he came back here for good, it would be as if he'd never left.

HUGH WAS PLEASED to find that the routine tasks came naturally. He was an ace at making coffee, asking new arrivals to seat themselves and refilling the napkin and condiment dispensers on the counter.

Dealing with the customers themselves was another matter.

His first faux pas occurred when a chunky man in his forties ordered a couple of doughnuts to go and Hugh handed him a bill.

"What's this?" the man said.

"That's two doughnuts at seventy-five cents each," he explained.

"I've seen you here before, haven't I?" The man eyed him suspiciously. "In fact, if I recall correctly, you got in some kind of trouble."

"Me?" Hugh said.

"You think maybe I'm talking to the wall?" was the sarcastic response.

Hugh was wondering if he'd run into the town troublemaker when Judy hurried over. "There's no charge for the doughnuts, Chief Oblado."

Chief. As in police chief? The man was wearing a suit, not a uniform. "I'm sorry, I didn't recognize you," Hugh said.

Understanding dawned on the chief's face. "You're the guy that was missing, Meg's husband. I heard they found you. Quite a story."

"Yes, it was," Hugh said.

"I was suspicious of you when Sam first brought

you to town," the chief admitted. "Got to like you after a while, though. I'm glad to see you back."

"It's only temporary."

"Whatever."

After he left, Judy said, "We don't charge the chief. I like to have him come in here. It's a peaceful town but once in a while troublemakers drive through, and I like seeing his patrol car out front."

"Sorry. I forgot," Hugh told her.

"That's understandable," she joked. "Considering all the other things you forgot."

For the rest of the afternoon, he concentrated on re-filling cups of coffee and keeping his customers' orders straight. After each person departed, he scrubbed the counter with repeated applications of spray.

"Your customers aren't going into surgery," Meg told him as she scooted by with a tray of orders. "You don't have to sterilize the place."

"Sorry." It seemed that he was using that word a lot.

Hugh grinned to himself. What would Andrew say if he saw his brother taking orders for burgers and fries? Probably that it was what Hugh deserved.

After five o'clock, the coffee shop got busier. Vinnie Vesputo, the elderly man Hugh had met on his previous visit, planted himself at the counter and continued to sit there long after he'd finished eating.

"Since you don't remember me," he said, "I might as well tell you my life story again. At least I won't bore you. Unless you found my story boring the first time. Did you?"

"I'm sure I didn't," Hugh said.

"It began when I was a child," Vinnie said.

"What did?" Hugh wiped the counter.

"My life."

"You were never a baby?"

"I don't remember that far back," Vinnie said. "Maybe I have amnesia, too."

A woman with a pair of sunburned children entered the cafe. Hugh was about to direct her to a booth when the kids clamored to sit at the counter.

Wearily, she seated them on either side of her. Both youngsters, a boy about six and a girl about three, had bright sunburns.

"Spend the day at the beach?" Hugh asked, handing them menus. Holding hers upside down, the little girl scrutinized it solemnly.

"Yes. Everybody want hamburgers? Fine. That's what we'll have," the woman said.

Hugh wrote down their order and set it in the aperture for Sam. Although he was itching to warn the woman about the need for sunscreen, he knew he ought to mind his own business.

"I remember when the first automobile came to Mercy Canyon," Vinnie droned from his stool.

Hugh performed some mental math. "You can't be that old."

"I'm not," the man agreed. "I was testing to see how smart you are. Being a doctor and all."

"A doctor?" The woman wrinkled her nose skeptically. "I bet."

At the other end of the counter, a woman in a pink uniform looked up from reading a book and nibbling on onion rings. "I'm having a lot of lower back pain. I clean rooms at the motel, so it's a serious problem. What should I do about it?"

This wasn't a pediatrician's area, Hugh thought, but maybe he could help. "You need to do specially designed exercises to strengthen your back muscles. Also, make sure you're not bending from the waist or lifting heavy objects. Ideally you should have a complete workup.''

"That's what my doctor said," the woman muttered. Her name tag read Susan, he noticed. "I thought you might have some better advice."

His best advice would be for her to get a less stressful job, but she probably had no choice, Hugh thought, and maintained a diplomatic silence.

A few minutes later, the family's meals arrived and Hugh set the plates in front of them. "Are you really a doctor?" the little boy said. "My nose hurts from the sun."

"Put some mayonnaise on it," his mother responded. Her daughter giggled.

Hugh couldn't contain himself any longer. "You can buy topical spray to take away the pain temporarily. In the future, I hope you'll use sunscreen. Any serious sunburn during childhood increases the risk of developing skin cancer later."

"Oh, sure, like you would know!" the woman shot back. "You couldn't even fix that lady's back problems."

"I got sunburned every summer when I was a kid," said Vinnie. "Had to have some, whaddayacall'em, lesions removed a few years ago, so I guess the counter doc's right."

"Excuse me! We'd rather not hear your medical history while we're eating," said the mother.

Meg, slipping past to place an order, shot Hugh a sympathetic glance. His expression must have revealed his exasperation, he thought, and determined to keep his feelings under tighter guard.

It was odd, though. Normally, Hugh was known for playing his cards close to his chest. Only as Joe did he seem to reveal his emotions openly.

He felt more tuned in to the people around him than usual, too. From the way Judy limped, he knew her feet must hurt, and Meg kept flexing her shoulders from the weight of the trays. In the kitchen, Sam was whistling as he flipped patties, a testament to the man's good nature.

Distracted by his observations, Hugh wasn't paying much attention as he made change for the woman with back pain. "I gave you a twenty," she said.

"What?" He snapped out of his reverie.

"You gave me change for a ten."

He glanced down and saw that he had indeed set a twenty dollar bill atop the drawer. "I'm really sorry. I'm new at this."

"I can tell," she said, and stuffed the change into her purse before walking away.

"I certainly hope you're not a doctor," added the young mother. "You can't even make change properly."

"My receptionist handles the payments at my office," he responded. From her annoyed look, he gathered he wasn't likely to get a tip.

"Never mind," said Vinnie after the small family departed, leaving a single penny on the counter. "They may not appreciate you, but I do. Now, where was I? Oh, yes. I was sixteen when Pearl Harbor was attacked. Too young to enlist, but I lied about my age…"

More customers came in, and by the time the place emptied, it was nearly eleven o'clock. Even Vinnie had departed, apparently satisfied at having spun his rambling tale to the end.

"Closing time." Meg nodded approval at the polished state of the counter. "I can see you're ready."

"He isn't ready, he's compulsive," Judy grumbled, although she sounded more tired than annoyed. "Joe was never this neat."

"I can't help it," Hugh said. "I don't want to spread any germs. Isn't eleven o'clock a little early to close on a Saturday? Not that I'm eager to work later."

"It's a sleepy town," Sam called through the opening. "They roll up the main street in half an hour, so you'd better get on home."

Meg had a few more tasks to complete to ready her station for tomorrow morning's staff. Sam and Judy apparently worked again the next day, Hugh learned, and understood why the woman was so tired.

"She's proud of the coffee shop, though," Meg told him as they drove home in Hugh's sedan. "They bought it six years ago. It's been a struggle, but they're paying their bills, and that's as much as most people can hope for."

Hugh reflected on this comment. "I've always thought in terms of job satisfaction and shooting for my ideals rather than simply making ends meet."

"That's because you've never been poor," Meg said.

"It's true." He turned into the trailer park and found an empty slot. Eager as he was to see Dana, Hugh wanted to finish this conversation first. "It must be difficult not to have enough money," he said.

Meg released a long breath. "It isn't so bad for an able-bodied adult. As long as there are jobs, you have a choice, even if the choice isn't perfect. But when I was a kid and my parents were broke, there wasn't much I could do."

In the glow from a security light, she didn't look much older than a kid herself. Freed from the headband she'd worn at work, curls rioted around her face, and her mouth had a full, angelic sweetness.

"Tell me," Hugh said. "I'm sure your story is a lot more interesting than Vinnie's, although I did perk up during World War II."

Meg chuckled. "You know what? Being with you, it doesn't sting so much, thinking about the past."

He slipped an arm around her. Although Meg didn't pull away, she kept her face slightly averted. Not inviting him to make any further moves, Hugh noted.

"There's not much to tell," she said. "Tim and I—he's four years younger—had no one to take care of us when my mom suffered a breakdown. She was manic depressive."

"Couldn't your Dad help?"

"They divorced when we were little. He drank so much, most of the time he didn't even pay child support. So we got stuck in foster homes."

"Foster homes." He thought of the children he would be working with at the new project. Meg might be able to provide useful insights, if she didn't find the subject too painful.

Hugh was eager to tell about the new job, but this was no time to change the subject. "That must have been tough."

"It was miserable, even though most of the foster parents tried to be nice," Meg said. "We knew we didn't belong there. And sometimes we had to stay in other parts of the county, where we didn't know anyone."

"Yet you overcame it," he said.

"After Mom was diagnosed with bipolar disorder,

the medication kept her stable,'' Meg said. ''Things went well for a few years until she got cancer.''

A profound sense of empathy filled Hugh, and he tightened his grip on Meg, as if somehow he could go back through time and comfort the girl she had been. ''That was tough luck.''

''She died when I was seventeen.'' Meg stared through the windshield at the cool September stars. ''A friend helped me get declared an emancipated minor. I dropped out of school, landed a waitress job, and persuaded the powers that be to let me keep Tim.''

''They let you raise your brother?''

''He was mad at the world,'' she said. ''I was the only person who could keep him in school and away from bad influences because he trusted me. It worked out fine.''

This young woman had accomplished more as an impoverished teenager than most professional adults that Hugh knew. Not in terms of money or prestige but in essential human goodness.

''I'm proud of you,'' he said.

''Even though I dropped out of high school?'' He could hear Meg's uncertainty.

''Yes,'' he said.

She relaxed against his arm. ''Well...I guess we should go get Dana.''

''I guess we should.''

They collected the sleepy girl from the neighbor's place. Hugh insisted on paying for her care, then helped Meg tuck their daughter into bed inside her mobile home.

''I don't suppose I should sing,'' he said, gazing down into the crib.

"It's all right even if it's off-key," Meg said. "Although I know that frustrates you."

A sense of wonder enveloped Hugh at the realization that, although he hadn't to his knowledge sung in front of anyone in years, Meg must have heard him croon lullabies to their daughter.

"This really is my home," he said in amazement.

"The place where you can be yourself," Meg agreed.

"Even if I hit every note flat."

"Even if you fall flat on your face," she amended. "And throw every ball in the gutter."

Softly, he began to sing "Hush Little Baby," and took several bars to find the melody. Meg didn't even wince.

Chapter Ten

After opening the couch into a bed, Meg showed Hugh how to fix the sheets. They worked together smoothly. Despite his inexperience, he was a quick learner.

Her throat was still clogged with emotion from listening to him sing to Dana. And watching him bend over the little girl's sleeping form, lovingly touching her cheek.

Just the way Joe used to do.

She'd enjoyed watching him work at the diner, too. Even his mistakes were endearing. Although Judy had hidden her amusement, Meg could tell she'd gotten a kick out of him, too.

It was great the way he'd pitched in to help. There was nothing high-and-mighty about this doctor.

As she drew a case over the spare pillow, Meg tried not to think about how much she wished she weren't going to bed alone. It had felt natural to lean against Hugh in the car. She'd had to force herself not to show how much she wanted to kiss him.

It was late, and they were both adults. But it was too soon to invite him back into her bed, she conceded.

They needed to spend more time together. As much as possible.

Her gaze fell on a card propped on the coffee table. The front picture was a reproduction of a stunning watercolor showing a blossom-laden tree against a sunset.

"Joe," Meg said. "I mean, Hugh. Do you like watercolors?"

"I like that one," he said, following her gaze.

She handed him the card. "It's an exhibit of work by Lynn Monahan, my father's girlfriend. It opens next Friday in Los Angeles and I wondered if you'd like to go."

"Sure." He examined the invitation. "La Cienega Boulevard. That's where the top galleries are."

"I don't know about that," Meg admitted.

"You and your dad are on good terms?" He straightened the worn blanket on the bed.

"Yes. My brother still resents him for abandoning us, though," she said. "They've been estranged for years. Anyway, I'd like for you to meet him and Lynn."

Hugh nodded. "I'm looking forward to it. Dana can stay with my mother. I'm sure she'd be thrilled."

"I hadn't thought about going to your house." Although Meg liked the Mentons, the prospect of staying at their mansion didn't thrill her. "There's so little privacy."

"I know," Hugh said. "There's something else I wanted to talk about…" He paused as Meg struggled in vain to suppress a yawn. "Not tonight. We can talk tomorrow."

"About next weekend?" she asked, puzzled.

"About the future."

His words, and his obvious buoyancy, lifted her spirits. She was about to insist that they talk now, when another yawn seized her.

Morning, she decided reluctantly, would be soon enough.

ALL NIGHT, Hugh's body remained keyed to Meg's nearness. He pictured her lying beside him, rolling against him, touching him....

Each time they nearly joined, he woke up. First at 1:15 a.m., according to his watch. The second time at 3:22 a.m. The third time at 6:45, when daylight made it impossible to fall back to sleep.

He might as well not have slept at all.

There was no sign of Meg yet, but from Dana's bedroom came a soft babbling. Quietly, Hugh got up, pulled his bathrobe over his pajamas and went to investigate.

From the doorway, he could see his daughter sitting up in her crib. In her hands, a gray stuffed bunny hopped around her while she talked to it as if it were real.

Amid nonsense syllables, he caught words and names. "Peter Cotton...meet farmer...ow! ow!...run fast!"

She giggled and then repeated the scenario, taking delight in the beloved story.

"Good morning." Hugh came into the room. "What would you like for breakfast?"

"Doughnuts!" Dana dropped the bunny and lifted her arms to be picked up.

"Doughnuts? That's not a healthy breakfast," he chided, catching her against him.

"Want doughnuts," she said.

Last night, Meg had brought home a few pastries that would be too old to serve to customers today. "Do you eat them with milk?"

"Yes, milk," Dana said. "Daddy, change me."

"Change you? I like you just the way you are," he said.

"Not me," the baby said. "Diaper."

Oh, yes, her diaper. "I'm a pediatrician. I can handle that," Hugh assured her, and tried to reassure himself.

He often refastened diapers on babies after examining them. That was different from performing the job from scratch, he soon discovered. It took three tries and an exclamation of "Loose!" from Dana before he got it right. This was obviously one skill that hadn't come back to him yet.

"Practice makes perfect," Hugh told his daughter on the way into the bathroom so they could both wash their hands.

"Perfect," she agreed.

Afterward, she toddled beside Hugh to the kitchen. Doughnuts couldn't hurt this once, he decided, as long as they were consumed with milk. When he and Meg lived together again, it would be time enough to broach the subject of proper nutrition.

When we live together...

While making coffee, Hugh imagined the three of them living in an apartment in Orange. Meg wouldn't have to work. She could if she wished to, of course, or she could take Mommy and Me classes and play all day with Dana.

A few minutes later, he heard the shower running. When Meg emerged, she was dressed in jeans and a sweater, her hair forming a happy cloud around her sleep-softened face.

"I'm glad you two had some time to get reacquainted," she said as she poured herself a cup of coffee. "How's it going?"

"Great." Hugh grinned at Dana, who beamed back from her high chair. "We have a wide selection on our breakfast menu today. Would you prefer jelly, lemon or chocolate-covered?"

Meg glanced at the smear of yellow on her daughter's face. "I'd say the lemon was already spoken for."

"I was hoping you'd pick jelly," admitted Hugh, who'd consumed both chocolate-covered doughnuts himself.

"You have a lot of nerve, offering me what you've already eaten!"

He assumed what he hoped was an expression of offended innocence. "The Back Door Cafe doesn't strike items off the menu just because they run out on one particular day, do they?"

"No, but we don't trumpet them to the customers, either!" Meg said. "I'll take—let me see—how about jelly?"

"A splendid choice, madame," he said, and presented the doughnut on a plastic plate.

On impulse, Hugh turned his chair backward and sat across from her. His feet landed right on the blackened patches of linoleum where his former self had worn through the surface.

It was time for her to move out of this dilapidated place. Long past time.

"I got the job I told you about," he said. "The project working with poor children."

Whatever reaction he'd expected, it wasn't blank puzzlement, followed by a forehead wrinkled in consternation. "You mean you're moving to Orange?"

"That's right," he said. "I'd like you and Dana to come with me."

He had intended to suggest that they get married. In

view of her frown, this didn't seem like a good time to raise the subject.

"I was hoping you'd think about what I said." Meg set down her half-eaten doughnut. "There's an office for rent here in Mercy Canyon. It used to belong to a dentist, so it might be suitable for a doctor. We have poor children here, too, you know."

She sat watching him hopefully.

She couldn't seriously expect him to give up this opportunity, could she? Hugh restrained himself from saying so aloud, reminding himself that Meg hadn't had time to get to know Hugh Menton or his dreams.

He supposed he didn't entirely understand hers, either.

"I know it would be an adjustment for you," he said. "But Orange isn't so far away that you can't visit your friends as often as you like. The project is exciting. I'll be able to accomplish so much."

From outside, someone rattled the front door. "Knock knock!" called a male voice, and then, "Why is this locked?"

"That's my brother." Meg stood up, her gaze raking across Hugh's bathrobe. "Maybe you should…"

"…get dressed," he finished for her. "Right away." Grabbing his overnight bag from the living room, Hugh headed for the bathroom.

When he came out, a red-haired young man was rolling on the floor with Dana while Meg dried their breakfast dishes. The newcomer glanced at Hugh and broke into a broad grin.

"Joe!" In a flash, he was on his feet, one hand extended.

Hugh shook it with as much enthusiasm as he could muster this early in the morning. "Tim, I presume?"

"You don't remember me?" Despite the fellow's manly frame, his crestfallen expression made him look like a little boy.

"Things are coming back to me slowly," Hugh said.

"I figured for sure you'd recognize me." Tim sank onto the couch, while Dana busied herself running toy cars along the coffee table. "I had this girlfriend Cassie that I asked you about. She was in a hurry to get married and have a baby, and you said I was only twenty-one and ought to wait."

"Did you take my advice?" Hugh folded himself onto the floor next to his daughter.

"Yes, thank goodness. She married some other guy two months later. I realize she didn't love me, she just wanted a meal ticket."

"I gave you the same advice but you didn't listen," Meg said, coming into the room.

Tim grinned with a hint of embarrassment. "That's because you're my sister."

Hugh gathered he'd been like a trusted uncle to Tim. No wonder the young man was disappointed at being forgotten.

As he studied Tim, a scene popped into Hugh's mind. He was climbing down from the cab of a pickup truck in a parking lot at night. From a nearby building blared country music.

"Did you take me out for beer one evening while Meg was working?" he asked. "To a country music bar?"

"Yes!" Tim's gray eyes lit up. "You do remember!"

"I guess I do," Hugh said, pleased that the small recollection meant so much to his brother-in-law.

Meg handed Tim the watercolor card. "We're going

to this exhibit next Friday. It features paintings by Dad's girlfriend Lynn. I was hoping you'd come.''

He handed it back. ''Give it up, sis.'' His face tightened, leaving no glimmer of his former cheerfulness. ''I don't want anything to do with Dad. He didn't act like a father when we needed him, and it's too late to start now.''

Hugh wondered if he should try to intervene. Tim hadn't asked for his advice, although from the pleading in Meg's face, she would appreciate an attempt.

''I was wondering,'' Hugh said. ''How old is your father?''

''How old?'' Tim repeated. ''I don't know.''

''Forty-seven,'' Meg said.

''And you're...''

''Twenty-seven,'' she said.

''So your Dad was twenty when you were born,'' Hugh said. ''Younger than you are now, Tim.''

The young man pressed his lips together before replying. ''I never thought of that.'' He shook his head. ''It doesn't matter. I'm not a drunk.''

''You mean an alcoholic,'' Meg corrected.

Tim scowled. ''I meant what I said.'' He changed the subject and began telling them about his most recent assignment, a trip to Albuquerque, so Hugh let the matter drop.

He was sorry his insight hadn't made any difference. He could only hope that he might have started the young man thinking in a new direction.

ALL WEEK, Meg missed Hugh intensely. Sometimes she thought she mostly missed Joe, but at other times she caught herself smiling at things Hugh had said, at his mistakes while working behind the counter, at his thoughtful comment to Tim.

She wanted her husband back. She also wanted Hugh, in a way that made her feel almost disloyal to Joe.

Driving to Los Angeles with her daughter on Friday, Meg finally pinpointed what the problem was. Despite her reservations, she was excited about Hugh's new job and the possibilities he'd outlined of a better future for Dana. He offered opportunities that Joe couldn't have given them.

Meg had treasured what she'd had with Joe, the safe, secure home she'd longed for. That had been enough for her, and in her plans for Dana. It ought to be enough now, she couldn't help thinking.

Enough for both her and Hugh. Why couldn't he just be Joe again?

Yet she was no longer sure that was what she really wanted.

"HERE." Andrew dropped a set of keys on top of the chart Hugh was reading. He barely caught them before they slid to the floor.

"What's this?" Hugh dangled them.

"Keys to the beach cottage," his brother said. "You and Meg need some time alone."

Andrew and Cindi's vacation home in Redondo was located within a half hour drive of the Menton home and also of the La Cienega art gallery. Staying there would allow Hugh and Meg the privacy they craved.

"That's a terrific offer. Thanks," Hugh said. "Do I take it you're not angry at Meg anymore?"

"Angry?" Andrew rubbed the bridge of his nose, massaging away the afternoon's tension. "I suppose I was at one time, but I can see she hasn't done anything wrong. I'm not pleased about you taking the university job, but that has nothing to do with Meg.''

"She's not crazy about it either,'' Hugh admitted.

"Why not? It's an honor.'' Andrew sounded slightly miffed. Maybe he was a little pleased about Hugh's achievements, after all.

Hugh glanced around to make sure they wouldn't be overheard. It was after five o'clock, and the only person he could see was Helen, finishing her charts at the front station.

"She had an idea that I might be willing to open a practice in her hometown,'' Hugh said.

"You're kidding! You, a small-town doctor?''

"It's not such a terrible idea, at least theoretically.'' Hugh felt obliged to defend Meg's position. "There's something cozy and old-fashioned about it.''

"You mean quaint and out-of-date.'' Andrew sniffed. "By the way, I ran into some of Dad's old friends at that luncheon I attended on Thursday.'' He was a member of several medical association committees. Hugh didn't know which one had held the meeting, nor did it matter.

"And?'' he prompted.

"They congratulated me about you taking on the project. Apparently they feel it's prestigious,'' Andrew said.

Hugh chuckled. "How ironic. I wasn't looking for prestige.''

"I know.'' His brother gave a rueful shrug. "All right, I'll admit, Dad would be proud of you. I just wish I could find someone to fill your shoes here. Permanently, I mean.''

"I'm putting the word out,'' Hugh said.

Sandy, the office manager, came by to lock up medications and make sure there were no stray charts or patients' belongings lying around. The solidly built, fiftyish woman wished them both a good weekend.

"You must be in a hurry," she told Hugh. "I understand Meg's coming to visit."

He glanced at his watch. "She may be at the house already. Just let me check my e-mail and I'm out of here."

"Go ahead. I'm not in a hurry to lock up."

He found nothing of interest in his queue. Certainly no response to his inquiry about the perfect doctor to take over his position.

After his brother's kindness in loaning him the cottage, Hugh wanted more than ever to remedy the problem he himself had created.

THE GALLERY featured works by three artists. One of the other participants painted dreamlike scenes in dreary hues, while the other made rusty-looking metal sculptures. Meg thought Lynn's watercolors were by far the best pieces.

She and Hugh only had a chance to say a few words to Lynn and her father when they arrived. Other guests intruded, and the small rooms quickly became crammed.

Tim wasn't there. Meg hadn't really expected him to show up, but she felt a twinge of disappointment as the closing time neared.

Hugh handed her a glass of wine. "You look like you need cheering," he said, warmth shining in his green eyes.

"I don't need wine for that," she answered, enjoying the sight of him. "Thanks, though."

An elegant blue jacket of textured silk brought out the vividness of Hugh's complexion and the sculpted breadth of his shoulders. From the corner of her eye, Meg noticed several women studying him admiringly.

She was glad she'd borrowed a dark gold body-skimming dress from Judy, which she'd worn with black high-heeled sandals. It had fit in perfectly at the French restaurant where he'd taken her for dinner, and it gave her confidence among the sophisticated gallery guests.

"Now that the crowd's thinning, I can see what an impact the watercolors make even at a distance," Hugh said. "If we were decorating a place, I'd suggest buying one."

Much as she appreciated Lynn's work, Meg wouldn't have considered paying over a thousand dollars for a painting. "Really?"

"It's special to own work by people you know. Assuming, of course, that they're talented, which she is." Hugh grinned. "Don't look so astounded."

"I'm sure they're worth the price, but I could think of a lot of things I'd rather do with that kind of money," Meg admitted.

"Consider it an investment," Hugh said. "Don't worry, I don't throw money around carelessly. I'd just like Dana to grow up surrounded by beautiful objects."

"I'll settle for appliances that work," Meg returned tartly.

"You can have those, too."

They drifted over to her father and Lynn. "Congratulations," Hugh said. "Your exhibit is a hit."

"I can't believe the response!" Lynn said. Tall and thin, with braided gray hair falling nearly to the waist of her India-print dress, she looked every inch the artist. "I've sold three paintings and a couple of people said they plan to come back for a second look."

"I'm not surprised," Hugh said. "Your work is exquisite."

Zack glanced up sharply as a gangly young man came through the door. At the sight of his unfamiliar face, the older man's shoulders drooped.

"I invited Tim," Meg said, guessing the direction of her father's thoughts.

"We sent him a card, too, so he definitely knew about the exhibit," Lynn told her. "Not that it matters for my sake. However, I hope he can make it to Zack's birthday party next month."

"It's my forty-eighth. It marks ten years I've been on the wagon." The older man gave Lynn a loving look. "Wonderful things have happened to me since then. More than I deserve."

"I'm glad," Meg said. She was also glad to see how healthy her father appeared, with his clear skin tone and his erect carriage.

"I wish I'd gotten my act together when you and Tim were kids," Zack said. "I used to make all sorts of excuses, blaming my parents and my susceptibility to alcohol. The truth is, I was self-centered and took the easy way out."

"At least you recovered in time to help me when I needed it," Meg said. "I don't know what I'd have done these past few years."

"You'd have managed," her father said. "You're a survivor, kid."

The gallery owner stopped by to congratulate Lynn. A few minutes later, Hugh and Meg departed.

Outside, the October air was crisp. Although the gallery stood in a row of one- and two-story buildings, a short distance to the north they could see the high-rise buildings of L.A.'s Wilshire District.

Meg was pleased to find that she didn't feel uneasy about leaving Dana overnight with Grace. She couldn't remember ever sleeping away from her daughter, yet she knew Dana was safe and happy with Grandma.

Right now, Meg felt young and unconcerned and eager. For what, she wasn't sure.

FROM THE COTTAGE, Hugh could see an intense bowl of stars over the ocean and hear the rumble of waves half a block distant. Despite the fact that he'd nearly died in a boating accident, he found the noise soothing.

"There's a kind of peace near the water, isn't there?" he said, as he and Meg stood on the porch of Andrew's cottage gazing down a gentle slope toward the beach. "The scientific explanation is that the water generates negative ions, but that strikes me as inadequate. I think the phenomenon defies explanation."

In the streetlamp-brightened darkness, a bicyclist wheeled past. The white-haired woman pedaled calmly, going home or perhaps out on an adventure.

"To me, the ocean is like the future," Meg said. "Clean and empty, waiting for us to fill it."

"Or clutter it?" he teased.

The breeze tossing her hair, she gazed out pensively, not answering. Seeing her lost in thought was new to Hugh.

"You're in a reflective mood," he said. "Any particular reason?"

"I was thinking that you're right," she said. "We need to be careful not to clutter up the future with leftovers from the past. Including our fears."

"Like your brother's doing?"

"I didn't mean him," Meg said. "I meant me."

She was shivering, although she didn't seem to notice. Hugh unlocked the door and, at the touch of a switch, a Tiffany lamp cast a cheerful glow from the lace-covered front table. "I want to hear more about this, but not at the risk of you catching pneumonia."

"Thanks. I guess I am cold." As Meg stepped into the parlor, Hugh tried to see it through her eyes.

The cottage, built in the 1920s, had been lovingly restored with period furniture and a stained-glass window above the mantelpiece. Cindi, who had spent her entire married life in her mother-in-law's mansion, had lavished loving care on this small home of her own.

"It's beautiful," Meg said.

Hugh chafed lightly at her bare upper arms, trying to warm her. "What did you mean about fears from the past?"

"I'm scared of a lot of things," she admitted. "Moving away from Mercy Canyon, which is my home. Going to a place where I don't belong. I'm tempted to cling to whatever security I've found."

"That's because of your childhood, all those uncertainties while you were growing up." His hands slipped around her, stroking her back. Beneath his hands, the satiny fabric of her dress felt like bare skin.

"I'm proud of what you're going to be doing at your new job, Hugh," Meg said. "I'm willing to take a chance. And I know Dana will have more opportunities living in Orange County than in Mercy Canyon."

"I don't want to pressure you," he said. "But I'd love to have you both with me."

Her face tilted toward his, vulnerable and receptive. Her full lips parted and, moving against her, Hugh bent to explore them.

He cradled her in his arms and deepened the kiss, delighting in the way her tongue responded to his. Slowly his hands traced the back of her dress. Her body swayed until she fitted tightly to him and the tips of her breasts beaded against his chest.

Hugh could hardly breathe as wild longings fired through him. From the shallow rise and fall of her chest, he knew the same excitement surged inside Meg.

He longed to sweep away every barrier and every doubt between them. Without another word, he lifted her in his arms and carried her like a bride to the bedroom.

Chapter Eleven

Hugh's arms felt strong and safe as he lowered Meg to the bed. She longed to be a part of him, to join with him as she had with Joe.

She didn't want to wait for them to undress. Just the sight of him shrugging out of his jacket set off a hunger so powerful that she caught Hugh by his silken tie and pulled him down.

Grinning, he braced his hands on either side of her. "I wouldn't want to ruin your dress."

"My dress will be fine."

"Can I take my shoes off?"

"If you insist." Without waiting, Meg unbuckled his belt, remembering instinctively how to unwork it by touch. She knew so much about him, including how quickly he could elevate her past herself into a glorious world of sensation. She could hardly wait.

Laughing, Hugh kicked off his shoes. "You're some woman!"

"It's been two years. That's long enough." After fiddling with the buttons on his shirt, Meg gave up. "Oh, keep the darn thing on."

"Not so fast. I've never done this with you before,

or at least I don't remember it clearly," Hugh said. "I want to enjoy every minute."

She stared up at him in the faint moonlight streaming through the window. She yearned for the nip of his teeth against her breasts, for the hardness of him between her thighs, yet something held her back.

He didn't remember being her husband. Didn't remember the first time they'd made love, when she gave him the special gift she'd saved all her life.

And she was about to throw away their reunion as if it meant nothing more than momentary lust.

Although the heat refused to die, something inside Meg shrank back. "Hugh…"

He rolled down beside her on the bed as his hands feathered her dress up her legs. "If you insist, however…"

"Hugh!"

He stopped. "Did I miss something?"

"It's not your fault."

"What's not my fault?" He propped himself on one elbow. In the semidarkness, he formed a watchful silhouette.

"I just realized—I mean, making love means more to me than this," Meg said.

"More than being with a man who loves you?"

His words should have reassured her. They didn't. "You can't love me. You don't know me well enough."

"We were married!"

"Joe and I were married," Meg said. "You're only partly him."

A warning note crept into his voice. "I'll never be him completely, Meg."

"I didn't mean that," she said. "I mean, to you I'm

still a strange woman. Maybe you find me attractive…''

''That's an understatement!''

''…but you don't remember the stages of falling in love. We haven't had a chance to go through them again. At least, you haven't.''

Meg stopped, feeling miserable. Hugh had every right to be angry at her for leading him on and then stopping him cold.

''I'm not as concerned about the past as you are,'' Hugh admitted. ''Maybe I've become used to living with a blank space in my brain, although it's shrinking. I do remember quite a few things about us, more than you suspect. I don't think my amnesia is the real problem, though.''

''It isn't?'' Meg asked.

''The problem is that I have a rival and his name is Joe.'' With a sigh, Hugh sat up. ''You still love the old me, and your heart can't accept that I'm him.''

''I'm sorry.'' Meg didn't need to come out and admit he was right. They both knew he was. ''I'm especially sorry to be wasting our time alone.''

''You aren't wasting it.'' Hugh switched on the bedside lamp and began searching for his shoes. ''We wouldn't be having this intimate discussion at my mother's house, because we'd never have gotten this far.''

''So we're making progress?'' Meg asked.

''You said you might be willing to move to Orange with me. Did you mean it?'' He threaded his belt back into place. The simple gesture arrowed regret into Meg.

She'd made the right decision, though. She had to come to him without reservations if they were truly to begin again.

"I'm not sure." She wasn't ready to give up her job. Her nearness to Tim, her reliance on Abbie, the familiar sights and sounds of the mobile home park. "We need to take this one step at a time."

"We can start next weekend," Hugh said. "I'll be moving into my new apartment on Saturday and that evening there's a reception for the staff. I'd like you to attend with me."

It meant asking for yet another evening off from the cafe, but Sam and Judy understood what was going on in Meg's life. And the new part-time waitress would love taking over such a lucrative shift. "Sure."

"Tonight, I'll sleep in one of the kids' bedrooms," Hugh said. "Which reminds me that I need to bring in our suitcases."

"I'm really sorry," she said.

"Not half as sorry as I am." He managed to smile. "It's been two years of solitude for me, too. I missed you even before I knew who you were."

She was tempted to take him back in her arms. There was no sense in risking a repeat of her earlier withdrawal, though, which she knew was likely to happen. "A little longer wait won't hurt."

"That depends on your point of view," he teased. "Now I'd better get those bags."

Only after he left did Meg realize how cool the air felt and how restless the ocean sounded outside.

ON SATURDAY, Hugh awoke knowing there was one important thing he needed to do today.

"This morning, let's visit the gas station where I disappeared," he suggested as they breakfasted at a sidewalk cafe a few blocks from the cottage.

Nearby on the cement, a seagull pecked a fallen bagel. It ignored a couple of joggers trotting past.

Meg finished a mouthful of poached eggs before replying. "I was looking forward to a few leisurely hours of reading the newspaper."

"I can go alone if you'd prefer," Hugh said. "You'd be helpful, though, and I'd enjoy your company."

She wrinkled her nose. "I'm being a coward. Of course I want to be there."

"Although it might be painful to stir up those memories, it should be worth it." Hugh's mind raced over the same subjects it had covered all night as he drifted in and out of wakefulness. "Snatches of the past have been returning for weeks but I haven't been able to put them all together. Going to the place where I vanished might help us both integrate the pieces of the puzzle."

"Will it help me use big words like 'integrate'?" Meg joked.

"No, but it might make you more patient with my pedanticism," he said.

"I'd be more patient with it if I knew what the heck it is."

He regarded her wryly. "A pedant is a person who shows off his knowledge."

"I thought it was something you hung around your neck," she shot back.

A glow to match the October sunshine lifted Hugh's spirits as he watched his good-humored wife. Yes, his wife. That was how he regarded her, even though he knew she wasn't ready to assume that role again.

He was tempted to join in the relaxation she'd suggested. It would be lovely to sit with her on the front porch, sharing a newspaper and watching the world go by.

Lovely, but not productive.

"The trip is important," Hugh said, tearing his thoughts back to reality. "I need to know what really happened. Don't you?"

"Of course." Meg set down her coffee cup. "I never believed you just drove away."

"I wouldn't have left you and Dana stranded," he agreed. "Unless, I suppose, my old head injury caused some unexpected memory lapse. It's possible I forgot where I was and started driving, hoping something would look familiar."

"Then someone bashed you over the head and stole my car?" Meg scoffed. "You know, if we want to recreate the scene accurately, we should pick up my car at your house. It's the same one you were driving that day."

"Good point," Hugh said. "I suggest we leave Dana with Mom, though."

"Absolutely."

After breakfast, they drove his car to the mansion and explained their plan to Grace. She was more than happy to keep Dana for the day.

"She's having a great time," said the happy grandma, pointing to where Dana rocked gleefully on a brand-new hobbyhorse installed in the den. "Angela's invited two girlfriends to a pajama party and they're looking forward to playing with the baby. Why don't you pick her up tomorrow morning?"

Hugh glanced at Meg, expecting her to object. She didn't. "Thanks, Mrs. Menton."

"Be careful." Grace laid a hand on Hugh's shoulder. "Going back might trigger an unexpected reaction. The doctor couldn't predict the long-term effects of your injury."

"I'll keep an eye on him," Meg promised. "At least he doesn't have a third identity he can disappear into."

"I certainly hope not!" Grace said.

In Meg's car, she fished around in the back seat for a map. The one she produced was creased and frayed and, when she opened it, marked with the route to Santa Barbara in red ink.

"Did I do that?" Hugh asked, studying the thin red line.

"Yes," Meg said. "I used it a couple of times later when I went up to visit Dad and it always gave me a start, seeing your marks on the map. Somehow I never got around to replacing it."

"Good. The more authenticity, the more easily I can put myself back in my frame of mind that day." After studying the map, Hugh headed for the freeway.

Half an hour later, at Meg's direction, they exited at an off-ramp that looked familiar. There was no gas station at the bottom.

"Did they tear the place down?" Hugh's stomach twisted at the possibility that he might never be able to stir his recollections.

"No. This is the wrong off-ramp. Some of them look alike," Meg said. "I wish I could remember the name."

"Don't apologize. It's been a long time," he said, relieved, and got back on the freeway.

"Here!" she said a few minutes later. "This time I'm sure. That tree was here, although it's taller now."

Hugh took the ramp and, at the bottom, turned into a service station. It resembled dozens of others he'd seen over the years, yet shadows began forming immediately in the back of his mind.

A gas island stood in front, with a minimart in back.

A truck was fueling at a side diesel pump, and a couple of cars flanked the center island.

"Red sports car," he said impulsively.

Meg blinked. "That's right. There was a woman driving. She left while I was going inside." She caught her breath. "I didn't mention her to the police. Do you suppose she came back and was involved in what happened?"

Hugh struggled to summon more images. "I don't think so. It was just a flash I got when I saw the cars filling up." He stopped on the outside of the island. "Is this where we parked before?"

"Yes."

"You should get out," he said. "Like you did then."

"That's right, I did!" She sounded excited.

"You went to change Dana's diaper." Hugh wasn't certain whether he was recalling the past or making an assumption. He knew it was true, though, and her nod confirmed it.

"Okay." Meg opened her door and got out. He did the same.

One of the other cars departed. Hugh wished the other one and the truck would leave, too. "We were the only ones here, weren't we?"

She swallowed. "Yes."

It was coming back, bit by bit. "You have to go into the minimart like you did before."

Meg didn't move.

"Well?"

"I can't," she said. "What if you aren't here when I come out?"

They stared at each other across the roof of the car.

To a casual observer, her comment might seem preposterous. To Hugh, it made perfect sense.

"You must have been afraid of that at some level since you found me," he said. "That if we got too close, I'd take off."

"I guess I have," Meg admitted. "I didn't realize it consciously. It's hard to take that risk again. I can't tell you how shocked I was."

He wanted to express his sympathy. This wasn't the right time, though. "We need to concentrate."

"Of course."

Something bad had happened here, Hugh knew instinctively. "I didn't drive off. I didn't suffer a blackout, either. Something…someone…"

She kept silent.

It wasn't coming back. "Maybe if you go inside it will help."

"All right." Apprehension dimming her usual spark, Meg walked slowly away across the pavement. The second car started as she passed, and an irrational bolt of panic filled Hugh. What if it shot forward and hit her?

She meant so much to him. She and Dana filled his world.

I had these thoughts before. It's returning.

His heart rate speeded and his hands grew damp. He was afraid, Hugh realized. Afraid of returning to the past, even in his mind.

Something very bad indeed must have happened.

A few more strides and Meg entered the minimart. The car drove off, leaving only the truck sitting by the diesel pump. Its driver must have gone inside as well.

Hugh was alone. The thrum of cars along the nearby

freeway formed a kind of white noise, blocking other sounds.

Footsteps.

He whirled. No one stood behind him.

He felt a presence. Joe Avery, filled with joy and with apprehension, too. Hearing footsteps. Seeing someone approaching.

A young, rough-looking man. No, two of them, separating as they moved to box him in. One wore a baseball cap, the other a gray jacket.

A gun. He could see it, pointed at him. It almost seemed to be there now, as if the tableau had remained unchanged all these years. Waiting for him to come back.

Joe held out his wallet and his keys. The men weren't satisfied. They refused to leave him behind to raise the alarm.

Hugh's heart pounded. If Meg came out now and interrupted the robbery, she and Dana might be harmed.

That was why he'd complied with the robbers and driven off. To protect his family.

He could see Joe getting in the car. Wishing someone would notice and be able to explain to Meg what had happened.

Please don't let her think I abandoned her. Joe seemed to be talking to Hugh across time. *Please tell her what happened.*

A turquoise minivan pulled off the freeway and parked alongside the island. The fragile overlay of the past dissipated, leaving Hugh both shaken and relieved. He understood now. Soon, Meg would understand, too.

IT MADE SENSE that he had left under those circumstances, she thought, standing next to the potato chip aisle in the minimart and listening to Hugh. The only part she couldn't figure out is why neither she nor the attendant had seen anything.

Still, judging by Hugh's account, the whole scenario couldn't have lasted more than a minute or so.

Relief flooded through Meg. Hugh hadn't vanished the second time around, despite her irrational fears.

Here he stood, solid and sturdy in his windbreaker, his blond hair disheveled from the breeze and his green eyes alive with triumph. At last they both knew exactly why he'd left.

To keep her and Dana safe.

"Then what happened?" she asked.

"They made me drive south." Hugh frowned in concentration. "They got angry, I think because I couldn't give them much money. I have the impression they meant to kill me."

Meg gasped. She caught a curious glance from the store attendant but he quickly lost interest.

"We must have exited the freeway in L.A. I guess at some point I jumped out and ran," Hugh said. "I don't remember the exact sequence of events, but they shot at me. I must have fallen and hit my head."

"The car turned up at a train station a few hours later," Meg said. "It had been ransacked, not that there was much for them to steal."

"I'll call the police and tell them what I've remembered," Hugh said. "It probably won't do any good, but you never know."

"I have the name of the detective investigating the case." Meg got a rueful glint in her eye. "You know what? I'm still carrying his card in my wallet. I never gave up, did I?"

"Thank goodness, or you might not have found me," Hugh said. "I'll call him on Monday."

"You're taking this so calmly," she said. "I feel like screaming or hopping up and down."

"I'd prefer to do handstands," Hugh said. "I can't tell you how relieved I am."

"Why?" She was the one who'd been worrying.

"It occurred to me I might have acted irrationally," he admitted. "That I'd suffered a psychotic break because of my first head injury. If that was the case, there might be some risk of it happening again."

"But it won't."

"No, it won't."

They smiled at each other. "Has it all come back?" Meg asked. "I mean, about our life together, and Mercy Canyon, and everything."

Hugh weighed her question for a moment. "I think so. There are lots of images in my mind. I can see our wedding, or parts of it. I remember moving into the trailer and being thrilled to have a home. Marveling that you could possibly love me."

"You really remember being Joe." Hugh even looked more like his old self than he had earlier, Meg thought. Joe used to stand in the same casual manner, his legs apart and his hands in his pockets.

"I do feel more like him," Hugh said. "Before, memories came to me like shots from a movie. Now I feel the emotions connected to them. Joe and I aren't entirely merged, though. I still feel like he's a little apart, watching me."

"That will go away," she said confidently. "Now that you've taken the first step, I'm sure things will fall into place." From this moment on, they could truly begin again.

Hugh glanced out the minimart's front window at the sun nearing its high point. "Let's grab a gourmet lunch at this fine establishment and take it to the beach."

"Just us?" she asked.

"Absolutely," Hugh said. "We'd break my mother's heart if we reclaimed Dana now. Besides, I want you all to myself."

"You've got me," Meg said.

THE MINGLED SCENTS of suntan lotion and salt air formed a powerful aphrodisiac, Hugh mused as he lay on an oversize towel next to Meg.

On her stomach beside him, she had propped herself on her elbows while reading a novel. Bright sunlight picked out strands of copper and russet in her hair.

The dark blue swimsuit bared a stretch of smooth back, and, farther down, slim tanned legs. Hugh visualized her again emerging from the shower at the pool house, splendidly naked. Hot sensations pounded through him.

The irony was that he couldn't summon a specific recollection of making love to Meg when she was his wife. Only the certainty that it had been magnificent.

She stuck a marker in the book and cocked her head at him. "What is it?"

"You mean, why am I staring at you?" he asked. "Because you're beautiful."

Meg sat up and hugged her legs. "Thanks."

She didn't sound, or look, very enthusiastic, Hugh thought with concern. Judging by her body language, she was in a self-protective mood. "What's wrong?"

"I'm not sure who you are anymore," Meg admitted. "Once, you were Joe, and then you were Hugh.

Now you're some of each. It's starting to bother me a little.''

"This is confusing for me, too." He rolled from his back onto his side to face her. "Now that I have Joe's memories, I understand why you believed I would go back to live in Mercy Canyon."

"You do?" Hope trembled in her eyes.

Hugh hated to destroy her fantasy, but he hadn't changed his mind. It was best to let her down easy, though, he decided.

"As Joe, I was dazed and disoriented when I found myself a stranger with no memory," he said. "Your kindness and Sam's and everyone else's was a tremendous boost. I wanted to put down roots and never let go."

"And now?" Restlessly, Meg scooped sand into her palm.

"I think of Mercy Canyon with joy and relief," he said. "I've been Hugh Menton for thirty-three years, though, and I was only Joe Avery for eighteen months."

Sand trickled between her fingers. "There's a lot to like about Hugh Menton, even though I miss my Joe."

"So you do like me?" he teased.

Meg shot him a quick smile. "Sometimes."

"How about now?"

"I'll say this. You look every bit as good as he did in a swimsuit." Her gaze burned across his bare chest and stomach. Hugh's muscles tightened reflexively.

He wanted her with an almost painful intensity. "After a remark like that, Joe would challenge you to a race back to the cottage."

Her eyes widened in startled recognition. "That's right, he would have."

"He'd start by rolling you off the towel." Without

waiting for her reaction, Hugh scrambled up, grabbed the fabric and jerked it.

"Hey!" Arms flailing, Meg slid onto the sand. "That's cheating! I wasn't ready."

He grabbed the towel and their beach bag into a messy bundle, ignoring an inner voice that nagged him to shake out the sand and fold things neatly. "Let's go."

She flung a stinging handful of sand against his legs. When he bent to brush it off, she jumped up, grabbed her sandals and ran barefoot toward the sidewalk. "Last one home has to take off his clothes in the living room!"

An older man and woman sitting nearby on deck chairs glanced up from their newspapers. "That sounds like a good game," said the man.

"Don't you try it, you old fool," retorted his wife. "Hand me the crossword puzzle, would you?"

"How about if I promise to cook dinner tonight?" asked the man.

"Now, there's an interesting offer."

Hugh didn't stick around to learn how the discussion came out. He pelted after Meg across the beach.

At the road, she zipped across, just ahead of a stream of bicycles. They blocked Hugh's path, so, by the time he arrived at the cottage, Meg was already standing on the porch.

"I win!" she crowed.

"Promise we can draw the curtains," he said, laughing.

"If you insist."

They shook off sand on the porch, then went inside. Hugh's sense of fun dimmed as he entered his brother's tidy cottage.

"We should take a shower first," he said.

Meg dropped the towel on the carpet and kicked it open. "You can stand here if you're worried about the sand falling out of your trunks."

Hugh's cheeks heated. "You don't really expect me to perform a striptease, do you?"

In answer, Meg pulled the cord on the front blinds, throwing the bright room into twilight. "You're safe from prying eyes now, Doc."

He couldn't believe he'd let himself in for this. Or, rather, that Joe had let him in for this.

Yet he liked the Joe-side of his personality. The guy was playful and bold. Unfortunately, it was Hugh Menton who had to strip.

"Well?" Meg folded her arms, a motion that squeezed her breasts into inviting round orbs above the low neckline.

"You didn't say I had to do it alone." Hugh caught her hands and pulled her onto the towel with him.

"Wait a minute!"

He slid the straps down her arms, baring her breasts almost to the tips. "That's a lovely sight."

"Cheater!" Laughing, she grabbed for his waistband.

"This kind of cheating feels so good." He stroked down the swimsuit top and bent to catch her nipples with his lips.

Wiggling, she grasped the ties securing his trunks and unworked them. Hot desire raged through him as her fingertips caressed his hips below his loosened waistband.

At the same time, Hugh's tongue trailed over the budding tips of her breasts. They both teetered on the edge of losing their balance.

"We ought to lie down before we fall down," Meg rasped.

"Don't let go of me," Hugh said. "Together now. One, two, three…"

They sank down, doing their best to strip each other as they went. At the last minute, Meg hooked her ankle around Hugh's and sent him tumbling onto the towel.

"Got you pinned!" She straddled him, pushing his wrists toward the floor. The sight of her bare torso poised above him sent his hormones into overdrive.

"That's what you think." With one powerful twist, Hugh rolled her onto her back and braced himself atop her.

"No fair!" Meg squawked.

"Isn't it more fun this way?" he teased and, at the same time, yanked her swimsuit down her legs and tossed it aside.

"You were supposed to take yours off first!" she said in mock protest.

"Who cares?" Hugh asked, and claimed her mouth with his own.

She kissed him back, deeply and passionately. At the same time, she pushed down his trunks and grasped his hips, positioning him over her.

He couldn't believe she was ready for him. His Meg. He remembered how cautious she'd been the first time, and how eager, once aroused.

In some ways, she'd still been a girl on their honeymoon. Now she was completely a woman, the only woman Hugh had ever truly wanted.

He fumbled in a drawer and, mercifully, found some protection. When he entered her, primal male instincts overwhelmed Hugh's self-control, transforming him into a fierce but tender lover. Beneath him, Meg grasped his buttocks, uttering little cries as she slid along his hardness.

Hugh groaned at the keenness of his pleasure. He wanted to prolong this sweet moment of rising joy.

The pressure of her soft bosom beneath his chest, the moistness of her mouth and the insistent stroking as he thrust in and out of her left no room for delay. An explosion rocked Hugh, launching him into a realm of pure bliss.

Meg shuddered ecstatically with him for several wonderfully long moments. Then they lay in each other's arms until the cool air roused them and sent them, chuckling at their own impulsiveness, to the shower.

Chapter Twelve

As hot water sluiced over her, Meg knew she was standing on the brink of a new life. Making love to Hugh had marked a commitment on her part, although she hadn't yet sorted out the implications.

"We should get married again," he said, soaping up her back.

Meg gave a little start that nearly sent them both slithering into the tiled wall of the shower. "What?"

In her mind, a tiny voice demanded that she give him a more direct answer. Like "Yes!"

He was Joe, after all, and they loved each other. Yet something wasn't quite right.

She had to know, beyond any doubt, that the two of them could live happily together for the rest of their lives. So far, she hadn't reached that point.

"I guess these aren't the conventional circumstances for a proposal," Hugh said, laughing. "In my own defense, let me point out that if I get down on my knees, the spray will hit me right in the eyes."

Meg took a playful swipe at his hair. Even laced with water droplets, it felt soft.

"There are a lot of things we haven't resolved," she reminded him. "Such as where we're going to live."

"I thought I explained that the project is arranging for me to rent an apartment in Orange County," Hugh said.

"I didn't mean the exact location," Meg said. "I meant that I'm not ready to give up my life in Mercy Canyon lock, stock and barrel."

"Give up your life?" Moving behind her, Hugh clasped her in his arms. The masculine length of him pressed deliciously against her back. "I should think you'd view my proposal as exactly the opposite. It means we're both getting our lives back."

Meg rested her head against his chest as water trickled between her breasts. "I need to take this one step at a time, Hugh."

"Next Saturday night will be a start." His voice rumbled through her. "At the welcome reception, you'll get to meet my new colleagues and see where I'll be working."

"I'm looking forward to it."

"Come early and we'll cook dinner at my new apartment," Hugh said. "I mean, at our apartment."

Meg's chest squeezed as she visualized modern, empty rooms. Empty not only of possessions but of memories. How could she leave her trailer, rundown or not, when every square foot reminded her of the precious time she and Joe had spent there?

Joe was back, she reminded herself. There was no more need to console herself with memories.

"Just give me the address," she said. "I'll be there."

ALL WEEK, Hugh had a hard time not whistling while he worked. Only the sight of his brother's less-than-joyful expression kept his high spirits in check.

He regretted leaving Andrew to shoulder the burden of their practice. However, with the retired pediatrician ready to step into his shoes, the situation wasn't urgent.

In most ways, the world seemed a bright and merry place.

Hugh and Meg had made love three times on Saturday night. Then, on Sunday, they'd taken Dana to the beach. Slathered with sunscreen, their daughter had romped in the surf with Hugh and dug a hole in the sand halfway to China.

Despite Meg's reluctance to marry him again, she had relaxed on Sunday. She just needed time to get used to the idea of moving, he thought.

The clouds that had darkened Hugh's world for the past two years were gone. His life made sense, now that he had regained his memory.

On Monday, he'd called the Los Angeles police to tell them what he recalled. The detective, after digging out the case, advised him that two men had been identified by an informant as having robbed a man on that date and left a stolen car at the train station. They hadn't been prosecuted because, without any witnesses to link them to Hugh, there wasn't enough evidence to take them to court.

However, both suspects had since been convicted in another armed robbery and attempted murder case, and were serving long sentences. Hugh's information would be turned over to the district attorney but the detective doubted they'd be prosecuted.

"As it stands, both were sentenced under the Three Strikes law. By the time they get out, they'll be ready for Social Security," he said.

"Fine with me," Hugh said. "As long as the public

is safe from them, I'm satisfied.'' He was relieved not
to have to drag Meg through a trial.

By Friday, Hugh felt like a kid awaiting recess as
he planned his move to Orange County the next day.
In the afternoon, though, his reverie was interrupted by
childish shrieks coming from the waiting room.

Concerned, Hugh strode down the corridor. Although Andrew always contended it was the staff's job
to handle nonmedical matters, Hugh worried too much
about his patients to stand by when something might
be wrong.

Besides, Helen Nguyen was busy weighing a baby.
The office manager, Sandy, had stayed home with
stomach flu rather than risk infecting others, so Chelsea
was alone with the phones and the arriving patients.

When Hugh opened the door to the waiting room,
the howls got louder. Three mothers waiting with their
children glanced up with varying degrees of exasperation as a fourth struggled to stop her three-year-old
twins from bashing each other with toys.

''They're wild from exhaustion. They kept each
other awake all night,'' she explained. ''And me, too.''
Dark shadows haunted her eyes.

''Chelsea?'' Hugh turned to the receptionist's
counter. ''Do you have a couple of those sugar-free
lollipops?''

''That's bribery!'' said the receptionist, whose hair,
he noticed, had purple streaks in it this week. ''Actually, I approve of bribery. Maybe I should run out for
ice-cream cones.''

''They'd drip it all over the place,'' sighed the fraz-
zled mother. ''Lollipops would be fine. I usually carry
candy for emergencies but we used it earlier.''

Peace was restored as both boys sat on a couch, licking their treats. Hugh also gave suckers to the other waiting children. "They deserve a reward for *not* misbehaving," he explained to Chelsea as he returned to the inner office.

"It was such a simple solution!" she said. Up close, the receptionist had delicate features, Hugh noticed, although with her spiky hair and heavy makeup, it was hard to tell. "I'm glad I don't have kids. I completely lack mothering instincts."

"Don't you want children?" he asked.

Chelsea shrugged. "First I'd need a father, and when it comes to men, I tend to pick losers. I'm better off alone."

A short time later, she buzzed his office to notify him of a personal phone call. As he picked up the receiver, Hugh looked forward to talking to Meg, whom he assumed was his caller until he heard a baritone voice.

"This is Barry." In the background over the phone, Hugh detected a babble of voices and what sounded like a bleating goat. "I wanted to make sure you got my answer to your e-mail."

"About the job?" It had been a good idea to contact their cousin about replacing him, Hugh mused. A workaholic and an excellent doctor, Barry was ideally suited to working with Andrew, and, as he was wrapping up two years in the Peace Corps, he needed to join a practice. "I didn't receive anything from you."

"Oh, heck," Barry said. "I wrote it off-line, and it must have been wiped out when the electricity died. Anyway, I'll be delighted to work with Cousin Andrew."

"You're coming? That's great!" Hugh said. "What can I do to help?"

"Nothing. I've arranged with an online real estate broker to find me a place near the beach." Barry was, as always, the soul of efficiency. "The earliest I can come will be in March. Is that okay?"

"We'll take you when we can get you," Hugh said.

"I'm eager to see Aunt Grace and the rest of you. It's been far too long."

Barry had intended to make it back six months ago for his mother's funeral, until a deadly storm pinned him down. The next day, after it passed, he'd called to say that, with many children injured, he couldn't leave his post. Hugh was certain his aunt Meredith would have agreed with her son's priorities.

"It'll be great having you here." As Hugh spoke, the background bleating grew louder. "What's going on?"

"Some people want me to examine their goat," Barry said. "My orderly is trying to persuade them to leave."

"Don't they know you're a pediatrician?"

"They claim the goat is like a child to them. As if that made any difference!" He laughed. "It's going to be interesting, getting back to civilization. Do they still have unmarried women out there? I haven't dated anyone in ages."

"Millions of them," Hugh said.

"I'm looking forward to meeting them," said Barry. "After so much time in the middle of nowhere, I hope I don't act like an ape man."

"I'm not sure some of the women around here would notice," Hugh said, recalling descriptions Chelsea had given of the wild behavior at the clubs she frequented.

The bleating intensified, and the background voices

rose to a fever pitch. Amid the cacophony, Barry said a quick goodbye and hung up.

With a smile, Hugh went to notify his brother that the problem of finding a new doctor had been solved.

ON SATURDAY afternoon, the diner was empty except for a few regular customers when Rosa dragged Meg inside. They were pushing Dana in a stroller and carting three outfits borrowed from the local boutique, Dressy Lady, because they couldn't agree on a choice.

Judy shot them a bemused expression. "What's this?"

"We want your opinion about what she should wear tonight," Rosa said.

"She's crazy," Meg told Judy. "I am not modeling those dresses in here." She was beginning to wish she hadn't decided to take a friend with her to the boutique. Usually helpful, Rosa had only complicated matters this time.

"Don't try them on. We can hold them in front of you," said the hairdresser. "Now, doesn't this color look wonderful on her?" She rippled a low-cut, slinky emerald gown in front of Meg.

"It's too revealing," Meg said.

"If I had your figure, I wouldn't wear anything else, even to bed!" Rosa replied.

Ignoring them, Tim set down his iced tea at the counter and came to pick up Dana. "How's my girl? Someday I'm gonna have kids but I doubt they'll be as cute as my niece."

"I doubt they'll be as cute as her mother, either," said Vinnie Vesputo from his seat. Despite his eighty-something years, the coffee shop patron hadn't lost his appreciation for women.

"What's the occasion?" Susan, a maid at the Mercy Motel, regarded them over her coffee cup from the opposite end of the counter.

"She's going to a party with a bunch of important doctors," Judy explained. "They work for a university."

Susan clinked down her coffee cup. "Don't tell me that guy who filled in for Miguel really is a doctor?"

Rose, Meg and Judy nodded.

"Oh, shoot!" Susan said. "I could have asked him for all kinds of free advice. A doctor!"

"He used to be a normal person," Vinnie told her, "until he got hit on the head."

The doors from the kitchen swung open and Sam emerged, rubbing his hands together. "You can't make any decisions without me. Show me the dress."

Rosa made another pass through the air with the emerald gown. Sam sighed. "It's sexy but it's not Meg's style. She needs to feel comfortable."

"Thank you." Meg was grateful for her employer's understanding of women. No wonder he and Judy were so happy together.

"Which one do you like, sis?" Tim asked.

"This one." She lifted a dress with a simple black bodice and a russet and dark green, leaf-printed skirt.

"Black doesn't flatter you," said Rosa.

"That print is appropriate for October, though," Susan commented.

"What else have you got?" asked Judy.

They produced a third outfit, which the saleslady had recommended. A slinky pants set in dark blue, it had a diamond-shaped cutout on the chest.

"Now, that's sophisticated," said Susan.

"How, uh, how low does that diamond thing go?"

Sam eyed it suspiciously. "Are we talking cleavage here?"

Meg nodded. "I want something more modest."

"If I had your bust, I'd show it off," Rosa said.

"Here's the solution," said Vinnie. "Meg gives you her figure and her bust, and you go to the party naked."

"Suits me if she goes in my stead," said Meg. "I'm scared to death. What am I going to talk about with medical people—the time I had my tonsils removed?"

"Ask them what I should do about my back," Susan said.

"You people aren't helping!" Rosa hoisted all three selections. "Pick one."

"There's nothing to discuss," said Sam. "Meg wears the dress she wants."

"Black doesn't go with red hair," Rosa muttered. "You're a guy. You wouldn't understand."

Sam, whose brown hair was thinning and receding, struck a girlish pose. "Of course I understand," he said in a high voice. "I wouldn't dream of wearing a dress that didn't flatter my beautiful long locks."

Everyone chuckled. "What's the big deal?" Tim asked, bouncing Dana on his shoulder. "These are just people. Why make such a fuss about them?"

Meg wished she had her brother's unflappable confidence. He enjoyed driving a truck and never seemed to wish he held a more prestigious job. However, at least he'd earned a high school diploma.

A rush of pride swept through her. She'd been scarcely more than a kid herself, but she'd done the right thing by raising her younger brother. That had been as great an accomplishment as becoming a doctor or a lawyer.

"You're right, it's not a big deal," she told Tim.

Turning to Rosa, she added, "You're right, too. Green is my best color and I can wear a showy dress if I want to."

"You really do like it? You aren't trying to spare my feelings?" asked her friend.

Wearing a knockout outfit would be a way of declaring herself the equal of any of Hugh's new colleagues. "Sure. I'm as good as anyone. Why should I hide behind something modest?"

"I like the green one best, too," Sam admitted. "I wanted you to feel right, though."

Relieved at having made the decision, Meg collected her daughter and turned to leave. With so much support from her friends, what could go wrong?

HUGH'S NEW APARTMENT occupied the second floor of a large 1920s craftsman-style home that had been divided into two rental units. An outside staircase led up to the private entrance.

Shouldering open the door, he edged inside carrying two bags of groceries. He hoped the pots and pans Hannah had provided him would be enough to cook dinner. He didn't want to buy kitchenwares, since he hoped Meg would be moving in soon with all her stuff.

From the sacks, Hugh retrieved salmon steaks, packaged scalloped potatoes and salad makings. This marked the limit of his cooking skills.

Possibly the extreme outer limits, he conceded, eyeing the wrapped package of fish. When the instructions said, "Broil," exactly what did that mean? Thank goodness Meg would be here to help, he thought, and stowed everything away.

With a few minutes left before her scheduled arrival, he walked through the apartment. Meg ought to like the picturesque bungalow style, similar to that of Andrew and Cindi's cottage although it wasn't nearly as well decorated.

He didn't think she would mind the eclectic selection of furniture, which he'd rented along with the unit. Hannah had insisted on cleaning the place herself, so it was spotless.

At the front window, Hugh opened the curtains to gaze down at the tree-shaded street. Most of the residents, he'd been told, were connected with either Pacific West Coast University or nearby Chapman College.

Some of his neighbors might be among the colleagues at tonight's party at the Faculty Club. In addition to physicians, he expected to meet nurses, psychologists and social workers, all committed to using their skills for the benefit of at-risk children. The conversation ought to be brisk and exciting.

Unexpectedly, Hugh felt disoriented. What was he, Joe Avery, doing with a bunch of intellectuals? People told him he was smart, but for Pete's sake, he'd dropped out of high school.

His fists tightened. This was crazy. Yet for a dizzying moment, the only memories he could summon were of going fishing with Sam and visiting a country music club with Tim.

Shaken, Hugh retreated into the kitchen and fixed himself a cup of instant coffee. Of course, he knew he wasn't Joe, or, rather, that he didn't have Joe's blue-collar background.

Into his mind, he summoned reassuring images. Andrew and their office. The hospital where he'd done his residency. A little boy he'd treated recently, whose symptoms he'd recognized as an unusual hereditary condition. Hugh had caught the case early enough so that, with proper treatment, the child should lead a normal life.

Although his confusion faded, the insecurity didn't entirely dispel. Hugh recognized it, not from his brief stint as Joe Avery but from his own teenage years. One semester when he'd received a B in biology, he'd been filled with the dread of not being able to live up to his father's expectations.

No wonder he was nervous. After a rocky series of experiences during the past four years, Hugh was entering a high-achieving group whose opinions mattered to him very much. He didn't want to let them down.

Well, since recovering his identity as Hugh Menton, he'd met everyone's expectations, including his own. Otherwise he would never have been hired for the Whole Child Project. There was nothing to worry about.

Recovering his aplomb, Hugh took down a cookbook Hannah had given him and began reading about how to broil fish.

WALKING THROUGH the parking lot toward the Faculty Center, Meg drew her lacy shawl tightly around her shoulders. A cool wind stirred the October evening as they approached the tree-lined walkways and textured-concrete buildings of Pacific West Coast University.

Hugh, lost in thought, didn't put an arm around her or notice her discomfort. He was walking so fast she could barely keep up in her high heels.

He'd been distracted all evening, unfortunately for both his culinary skills and the conversation. The fish had been slightly burned and the potatos clumped, while several times during dinner he'd simply stared into space.

Meg wondered if he disliked her dress. He hadn't said anything when she arrived, although normally he would have responded with a long look or an even longer kiss.

In his dark silk suit with a designer tie, Hugh made a stunning appearance. When he'd taken off his apron to sit down to dinner, she'd yearned to smooth her hands across his chest and muss that perfect blond hair a bit. But she was reluctant to touch him when he seemed so unresponsive.

As they exited the parking lot, his pace picked up, and the gap between them widened. "Hey!" Meg called.

He stopped a couple of steps ahead. "What? Oh, Meg, I'm sorry. I wasn't paying attention." He waited while she caught up.

"Is something bothering you?" She'd never seen him this edgy before. "Don't tell me you're nervous about meeting your new colleagues. They aren't any more special than you are."

"I'm not nervous." Hugh gave her a lopsided grin. "Excited, maybe."

"Well, I'm nervous," she admitted.

This time, he did loop his arm around her waist. The gesture sent warmth radiating through her. "You'll be fine. I hope you won't find the conversation boring."

"I promise not to ask them what to do about Susan's back problems," she said.

"Excuse me?"

"The maid from the Mercy Motel. She was sitting at the counter when you helped out, remember?"

Hugh blinked as if snapping back to the real world.

"Right. I'm sorry her back still hurts. Feel free to ask if anyone has a good suggestion."

"Hugh, I'm joking," Meg said. "I wouldn't ask these distinguished people about a backache."

"I don't see why not. Back pain can be debilitating." To her relief, he sounded like the old Hugh again. Or, rather, like Joe, she reminded herself.

Joe seemed to be slipping away, more and more. On this college campus, Meg could hardly recall him. Perhaps that was because Hugh belonged here, while Joe would have felt as awkward as she did.

They followed a walkway across the lawn. Meg spotted a man and two women heading toward the Faculty Center from the opposite direction.

The man and one of the women wore jeans. The other woman, tall and elegant with upswept hair, sported a business suit and low-heeled pumps.

A sinking sensation made her clutch her shawl tighter. She was hopelessly overdressed and likely to stand out like a sore thumb.

This was going to be even worse than she'd feared.

Chapter Thirteen

Inside, the low, modern Faculty Center hummed with voices. People gathered around a refreshment counter and sat on couches, talking intently.

The clothing styles ranged from strictly casual to businesslike. A couple of women wore party outfits, although none as showy as Meg's.

Remembering her friends' compliments, she straightened her shoulders and lifted her chin. Several men studied her admiringly, which cheered her a little.

If only Hugh would pay her the same attention! Instead, he was busy shaking hands with a man and introducing himself and Meg. The man welcomed them and directed them to a hospitality table.

"Dr. Menton?" asked a middle-aged woman seated behind it. "Here's your name tag. Oh, dear, I didn't realize you were bringing your wife."

Meg waited for Hugh to correct the mistake. "We can use one of these blank ones," he said, and wrote *Meg* on it in large letters.

Apparently he didn't intend to comment on their marital status. Considering how hard it would be to explain that she'd been married to his alter ego, Meg supposed his decision made sense.

The paper name tag, rimmed in Halloween-y orange and black, looked hideous stuck to her emerald gown. Meg suppressed a mischievous urge to slap tags all over her front and her forehead. That way people might not notice she'd come outfitted for a senior prom instead of a faculty party.

At the refreshment table, she discovered she was hungry. During dinner, she'd mostly rearranged the overcooked food on her plate, so Meg helped herself to a sampling of stuffed mushrooms and Camembert cheese.

She had a cheese and cracker bite halfway to her mouth when the tall woman they'd seen outside marched toward them. The woman carried herself with stiff authority.

"Dr. Menton?" She spoke with a slight Russian accent. "It's good to see you again."

He shook hands. "You should call me Hugh, Dr. Archikova."

Her expression softened. "Of course you can call me Vanessa, now that we're working together."

"I'd like you to meet Meg," he said.

The woman gave a nod of acknowledgement without taking her eyes off Hugh. "I apologize again for not getting back to you sooner. I'm glad you're here now."

"I'm sure we're all eager to get to work with the children," he said.

"The children, yes!" Vanessa's pale blue eyes took on new animation. "They have so many needs, it's been difficult to define our parameters."

"We'll be using a medical model, won't we?" Hugh said.

Meg wondered what a medical model was. She pictured an anatomically correct dummy with its internal organs visible through a transparent exterior, but doubted that was what he meant.

She decided not to ask. Better to reveal her ignorance later, when they were alone, or not at all.

Other people joined them, talking in more jargon. Several of them chattered so fast they were speaking over each other.

Meg supposed it wasn't unusual for co-workers to immerse themselves in shoptalk. At least, she thought wryly, these people operated on such a high conversational plane that they weren't likely to gossip about her inappropriate choice of a dress.

Finally the conversation reached a pause. In the silence, Vanessa addressed Meg. "Are you a doctor also, Mrs. Menton?"

The question caught her by surprise. Weren't the words *high school dropout* engraved on her forehead? Of course not, she chided herself.

"No, I'm—"

"She's been taking care of our daughter," Hugh said. "The most important job in the world."

"Absolutely," said Vanessa.

Anger at Hugh's half-truthful response swelled inside Meg. There was nothing wrong with being a full-time mother, of course, but she wasn't one, and he had no business acting as if he were ashamed of her.

"Actually, I'm a waitress," she said.

Vanessa opened her mouth but no sound came out. Perhaps she intended to make some pleasant comment. Obviously, she couldn't think of one.

A younger woman, who wore jeans and an embroidered overblouse, spoke up. "Your back must hurt. I earned my way through college waiting tables, and it was hard."

"It's not too bad," Meg said. "We've got a customer at my coffee shop who cleans rooms in a motel. Her back hurts all the time."

"Has she seen a chiropractor?" asked a man.

"I wouldn't think a bunch of doctors would approve of a chiropractor," Meg said.

"I'm a social worker, not a doctor," he said. "I injured my back in a car accident and without my chiropractor, I'd still be in pain."

Vanessa gave them all a vague smile, as if she had no idea how to participate in such a mundane conversation. "Well, there are a lot of people I haven't talked to yet. So nice to meet you, Mrs. Menton."

Meg nodded back, deciding not to explain that they weren't married. Judging by the strained look on Hugh's face, she'd said more than enough for one night.

A while later, they made a quiet exit. On the walk to the car, Meg kept waiting for him to say something.

She couldn't stand the suspense any longer. "You're mad, aren't you?"

"Not exactly." His voice bristled with tension.

"I don't believe in pretending to be something I'm not," she said. "There's nothing wrong with being a waitress."

"I didn't say there was."

Perhaps she ought to leave the matter there, but Meg couldn't. Hugh mattered too much for her to let an issue like this fester between them.

"I didn't mean to embarrass you," she said.

"I wasn't embarrassed."

"Yes, you were." When they reached his sedan, he unlocked it, but neither made a move to enter.

"Okay." Hugh ducked his head in acknowledgement. "I was a little embarrassed. Not because you're a waitress but because of the way you said it. Like you were confronting people."

The accusation startled Meg. "I was not!"

"You were challenging them to prove they aren't snobs," he said.

"You should have told the truth in the first place." She knew she wasn't fighting entirely fair. Still, he had provoked her.

"I wasn't prepared for Dr. Archikova's question and I wasn't sure how you wanted me to respond," Hugh said. "With an innocuous question like that, I couldn't call a time-out to confer with you before answering."

His answer made sense. Had she been wrong to speak up? Meg wondered. Or was he being less than honest about his own motives?

"Well, I am who I am," she said. "I'm a waitress who never finished high school. It's better that people know the truth right from the beginning."

"You don't have to define yourself that way." Hugh opened the door for her. "You can get a high school degree if you want to."

"That won't make me a professional like your colleagues." She eased into the car, trying not to wrinkle the dress, although that hardly mattered at this point.

Hugh came around and slid into the driver's seat. "Meg, you don't need to be a professional." Pale light from a streetlamp brought out his classic profile. "You're the equal of anyone there. You're the wife, or future wife, of a doctor, and the mother of my child."

"You mean I wouldn't be their equal if I weren't connected to you?" Although Meg didn't want to argue with the man she loved, she had to make him understand why she'd reacted the way she had.

"I didn't mean that," he said. "I meant that you don't need to wear your blue-collar past like a shield, or wield it like a sword, either."

"My past? I'm a waitress *now*. This isn't something out of the long ago." Tears stung Meg's eyes. Was Hugh truly ashamed of who she was? "I can't stop being the person I've been for twenty-seven years. Joe accepted me the way I was."

"It's time to get over Joe," Hugh said roughly. "For both of us. We have to live in this reality, the one in which I'm Dr. Hugh Menton."

"Your identity may have changed, but mine hasn't," Meg said.

His hands tightened on the wheel. After a moment, he started the car. "We both need time to cool off and think things over."

"I guess so," Meg said miserably.

She had arranged for Dana to stay overnight with Abbie, explaining that she didn't want to drive home alone at a late hour. Now Meg wondered if she should leave anyway. Certainly she and Hugh were in no mood to make love.

He must have been thinking along the same lines, because his next words were, "I'll sleep in the second bedroom. We can talk in the morning."

Reluctantly, she nodded. Maybe, she hoped, things would become clearer by then.

TOSSING RESTLESSLY in his narrow bed, Hugh wished Meg could accept that he wasn't Joe.

Joe had been grateful for any stability in his shifting world. Without a memory to anchor him, the job at the cafe and Meg's home in the trailer had come as a god-send.

Not that Hugh wasn't grateful for those experiences, too. Working at the coffee shop had provided security and close friendships.

He had even more joyful memories of the months he'd spent married to Meg. That had been the happiest time in either of his lives. Now, however, the two of them needed to adapt to their changed circumstances before they could find happiness again.

The flashback earlier this evening to being Joe had shaken Hugh. At the party, he'd had to struggle to fo-cus on the fast-moving conversation.

All evening, he'd had the sensation that Joe stood nearby, observing and listening. Trying to figure out what was going on and eager to return to a world where people placed few demands on him.

He thinks I'm still partly him. I'm not, though.

During the previous major transitions of Hugh's life, when he'd started medical school, during his internship and residency, and on first entering private practice, he had experienced a similar sense of disconnection, he recalled. It was as if he were an imposter who might get caught at any moment.

His experiences as Joe were merely an excuse that his subconscious mind must have fixed on tonight. The truth was that Hugh, like most people in transition, needed time to find his footing in this new phase of his career. Also, he needed Meg's support to help him get through this stage.

I am who I am, she'd said. The words were as true of Hugh as they were of Meg. He was who he was, and that man was not Joe Avery.

How long would it take her to accept the fact?

SHE HAD TO let him go.

It was the hardest decision Meg had ever made. Harder than dropping out of high school to take care of Tim, harder than marrying Joe Avery when everyone warned her to be cautious.

Although his new colleagues had been courteous, she knew she didn't belong among them. Agonizing as it was to admit it, she didn't belong with Hugh Menton, either. She would only hold him back.

That night, she slept restlessly, awakening often. Words and phrases turned over and over in her brain as she imagined how she would explain to Hugh that she was breaking up with him.

It might come as a relief. He couldn't really love her, because he didn't really know her. He loved a woman who looked and sometimes acted like Meg, but was fundamentally different.

He'd be happier with someone suited to his new environment. A woman who fit in, who felt comfortable with his friends.

It wasn't only a question of adjusting to the people she'd met last night or to this job in Orange. Marriage to Hugh meant going wherever he went, and he was a man on his way up.

In a year or so, there'd be another move to a different place. Another wrenching dislocation for Meg.

It meant suffering the same unpredictable losses she'd endured in childhood. She couldn't handle the tumult. The one thing she'd always dreamed of, a stable home of her own, would be gone forever.

The next morning, Meg got up early and showered. In the mirror afterward, she could see the strain on her face.

Okay, so she loved Hugh. But she couldn't live with him.

After dressing, Meg went out to fix breakfast. Although she had no appetite, Joe had always loved poached eggs and toast, so she set to making them. Maybe he and Hugh had at least that much in common.

While she was buttering the toast, the familiar creak of his footsteps approached. When she looked up, Hugh was standing in the doorway, shaking a rebellious wedge of blond hair back from his forehead.

A powder-blue polo shirt clung to his firmly built torso, above tight jeans that emphasized the slimness of his hips. Even at his most casual, though, she noted the details that distinguished Hugh from Joe: a designer logo on the shirt pocket, the ironed crease in the pants.

"'Morning," he said, his green eyes full of unspoken questions. "That smells great."

"Perfect timing. The eggs are done," she said.

Meg's throat clogged as she set out the food on plates. It was time to tell him what she'd decided.

HUGH KNEW he was in trouble. Meg wouldn't even meet his gaze.

Okay, he conceded silently, he might have to accept that she wasn't going to leave Mercy Canyon right away. It didn't matter. Sooner or later, they would work this out, because they loved each other.

She sank into her seat, misjudged the distance and dropped the last inch. The chair creaked.

"Trouble sleeping?" he asked.

Meg nodded. Defiant copper strands in her springy hair added emphasis to the slight movement.

"We didn't really fight last night, did we?" he asked. "We simply disagreed about a few things."

Hugh took nothing for granted, however. His brother had told him from long marital experience that sometimes a guy perceived things differently than a woman.

"No, we didn't fight." Meg released a long breath. "I'm not angry, if that's what you're asking."

"Good." Maybe the worst was over, he thought in relief.

"This isn't going to work," she said.

Hugh stopped with his fork halfway to his mouth. He didn't want to believe what he'd just heard. "What isn't going to work?"

"You and me. Or rather, Hugh and me." Meg poked at her egg. "Moving around in foster homes when I was young taught me that I need to find my place in the world."

"It's with me," he said.

"That's what I was hoping." She considered for a moment before continuing. "You need someone more like you. Maybe the right woman for you resembles me in some ways, but her background, her frame of mind, her tastes are different."

"You can change. I can change." He wished he could think of a more coherent response. He hadn't expected anything like this, so he wasn't prepared.

Meg couldn't simply write off everything between them. A marriage. A daughter. A future.

She shook her head. Her solemn face was pale beneath the sprinkling of freckles, making Hugh itch to reach out and take her hands for reassurance. She was clutching her tableware so tightly, though, that he feared he might get stabbed if he tried.

"You can visit as often as you like," she went on. "Dana needs her father. I would never stand between you."

"Whoa!" he said. "You make this sound so final."

"It is." Despite the glistening in her eyes, her chin thrust out determinedly. "It's better for everyone if we don't drag things out."

"We need a few days apart," Hugh said. "Time to calm down."

"I am calm," Meg said. "I don't want to prolong the agony. We only met because of a weird twist of fate. Now that fate has tossed us back into our original roles, you and I don't even belong in the same universe."

"We belong together, in every universe." Hugh felt like a man slipping off the face of a cliff, clawing for a handhold. There had to be a way to change her mind. He loved her too much to let her go. "Meg, from the moment you walked into my office last month, I knew there was something special between us, and that was before I got my memory back."

"Having special feelings isn't enough," she said.

"Both of us need to get accustomed to new ways of relating to each other. We need to grow and adapt, Meg."

Her hand trembled as she crumpled her napkin onto the table. "You talk about both of us adapting, but you mean me. I'm the one who has to change. And I can't. I'm sorry I can't be the woman you want me to be, Hugh, but it's better if we both accept it before everything falls apart and we end up angry and bitter."

She scraped back her chair and fled. Hugh decided to give her a few minutes to compose herself until they could continue the conversation on a rational basis.

Moments later, she returned carrying her overnight bag. She hadn't given him time to absorb everything she'd said, let alone formulate a response.

"Whoa." Hugh raised one hand in a stop gesture. "This discussion isn't over."

"Yes, it is." Tears brimmed in Meg's eyes as she struggled not to cry. Hugh's heart went out to her. "I'm leaving. Let me know when you want to see Dana." She flung open the side door.

He took a couple of steps in her wake, then hesitated. Since he didn't know what to say, he might only make matters worse.

Besides, Hugh realized, he was a little angry at her for being so demanding at this difficult time. If only she were willing to meet him halfway!

Maybe they did need some time apart.

Chapter Fourteen

On Tuesday morning, Meg vacuumed the trailer, scrubbed Dana's fingerprints off the doorjambs and walls, mopped the kitchen floor and baked muffins.

The place looked and smelled as good as possible. It still wasn't nearly nice enough for the visitors who'd called earlier and asked if they might drop by at eleven o'clock.

Grace and Cindi.

Hugh's mother had made the call. She'd just learned from her son that he and Meg had broken up.

"I don't intend to stick my nose where it doesn't belong," she'd said. "What's between the two of you is none of my business. But Dana is my granddaughter, and I hope you don't mean to keep us apart."

"Of course not! We'd love to see you," she'd said.

Now, dust mop in hand, Meg swept a spiderweb out of a high corner. Why hadn't she noticed before how dust managed to creep into every available space despite regular cleanings?

As Dana sang along with *Sesame Street* on TV, Meg hurried to the bedroom to brush her hair and reapply lipstick. A glance in the mirror showed that she had dust on her sweater, so she changed, then brushed her hair again.

Good heavens, she couldn't be more keyed up if Queen Elizabeth were coming to call!

Meg barely reached the living room in time to hear a light tapping. At the same moment, she realized she'd forgotten to put on shoes. Not wanting to keep her guests waiting, she took a deep breath and went to welcome them still wearing her fuzzy slippers.

The door opened to reveal patrician Grace, her silver hair perfectly coiffed, and an ill-at-ease looking Cindi, her hair twisted in a smooth French braid. Both women wore tailored slacks and blouses.

They'd probably conferred about what to wear. Meg could picture them discussing their wardrobes earnestly, and was touched to realize they might be nervous, too.

"Hi," she said, stepping aside to let them in. "I hope you didn't have any trouble finding the place."

"You gave great directions." On entering, Grace went directly to Dana. She plopped on the floor next to her granddaughter and regarded the TV. "Which one's your favorite? I like Big Bird."

"Elmo," said Dana, and gave her a hug. "Hi, Gramma."

Cindi gazed around as if seeking a topic of conversation. "What a nice…uh…that's a very interesting…uh… "

Meg had to laugh. "It's not a very fancy trailer. Still, I appreciate your good intentions."

Cindi released a long breath. "Thanks for understanding. I'm not good at making small talk."

Meg went into the kitchen to get the coffee and muffins. Cindi followed. "This is cute. Your own place."

"Thanks. Although it's not nearly as nice as your beach cottage," Meg said.

"I think it's wonderful how you've managed to support yourself and take care of your daughter." At her request, Cindi, who was taller, reached down a serving dish from a high cabinet. "I don't know how I'd have managed if my husband disappeared and I had to fend for myself."

"Don't be silly!" came Grace's voice from the living room. "You've got a law degree!"

She did? Although Meg had assumed Cindi had a college degree, she'd never guessed that Andrew's wife was an attorney. How peculiar that the woman still had to battle shyness!

"I couldn't work eighty hours a week and raise a child alone," Cindi answered.

"Do you think you'll ever go back to practicing law?" Meg asked.

"I doubt I'd want to work those hours even when my kids are grown," came the response.

"Not all lawyers work eighty hours a week. There's one here in Mercy Canyon who finds time to serve on the school board and take his kids to the park."

Meg arranged the muffins on the platter, wishing she had some curled orange peel to decorate them with. Although Sam had taught her how to make garnishes, she hadn't thought of it in time.

"I never thought of that," Cindi admitted. "Being in a small office might be fun. My family always assumed I'd land a prestigious position with a big firm."

They carried the refreshments into the living room. "Snobbery can be a heavy burden," commented Grace, who'd obviously been listening to their conversation. "Believe me, I grew up with it. Nothing was good enough for my father."

"You're not a snob." Cindi added cream and sugar to her cup.

"I hope not," Grace said. "The person I'm hardest on is myself."

"Me drink, too?" asked Dana.

"I'll get your cup." Meg hurried to fetch some milk from the refrigerator. Her daughter took the cup in two hands and drank through the small lipped opening.

They all watched *Sesame Street* for a while, laughing at the Muppets' antics. When Dana began to yawn, Grace happily carried her into the bedroom and sang her to sleep.

On her return, she removed a tissue-wrapped package from her large purse. "I hope this is the right size."

"We bought it a little large, to be safe," Cindi added.

Meg opened the tissue and held up a toddler-size yellow raincoat with a matching hat. "It's adorable! I'm sure it will fit. It's perfect for this time of year, too."

"It's been a long time since I had a small grand-child," Grace said. "I'd like to buy her lots of things, if you don't mind."

"That's very kind of you," Meg said. "You should feel welcome to visit without gifts, though. Dana needs her grandmother and her aunt."

"We didn't come only for her sake," Hugh's mother went on. "Cindi and I want to have a relationship with you, too. You're Dana's mother and you're a part of our lives now. We hope to be a part of yours, too."

"No matter how muleheaded my brother-in-law may be," Cindi added.

Meg wondered if she should admit that their breakup was her decision, not Hugh's. Neither of her visitors appeared eager to snoop or lay blame, so she decided to let the matter rest.

"I'm really glad," she said. "I don't have any close female relatives, aside from Dana."

They chatted for a while and, after Dana woke up, Grace took her for a walk. Cindi willingly helped Meg fold laundry. "Hannah does it so perfectly that I don't like to interfere, but I miss doing things like this for my kids."

"You can fold my laundry any time," Meg said. They both laughed.

By the time her visitors left, they had all relaxed. Both Grace and Cindi gave the impression that they'd thoroughly enjoyed themselves.

Without Hugh, Dana would never have had this chance to be part of an extended family. Joe hadn't had any close family, Meg thought with a twinge of guilt.

She hoped she wasn't being disloyal to Joe, to be so glad that their daughter at last had a grandmother and other relatives. If she hadn't lost him and found Hugh, it would never have happened.

Meg made a face at herself in the wall mirror. How silly could a person be? There was no Joe. There never had been, not really.

Why then, she wondered, did she still love him?

THAT WEEK, Hugh intended to think of arguments to change Meg's mind, but starting a new job and undergoing intensive training kept him fully occupied.

There were orientation sessions to attend. Social

workers, foster care workers, psychologists and school counselors to meet. A great deal to learn about how a doctor could screen for emotional and psychological needs during a physical exam, and which referrals to make.

All the while, a worry nagged at him. What if Meg had been right? Maybe he was kidding himself, believing they could make a home together.

It was possible she might never love him the way she had before, and there were limits to how much he could change to suit her. He wanted to meet her half-way, to adapt as she'd asked, yet he would never be happy working in a small office in Mercy Canyon.

Still, he fought against accepting their breakup as permanent. He missed Meg terribly. And he missed their daughter.

On Wednesday, Hugh called. "Let's try again," was the first thing he said.

"It won't work." Meg's voice trembled.

"There's no reason we can't take things slowly," he said. "We can compromise."

"Are you reconsidering my suggestion that you open an office here?"

At her hint of hopefulness, Hugh's chest constricted. He hated to disappoint her. "Meg, this project is a dream come true. I'm only sorry that it isn't located closer to Mercy Canyon."

Her low sigh reached him over the phone. "Hugh, let's not rehash the same arguments."

He'd lost this round. Hugh decided to accept it like a gentleman. "Okay. You did promise I could see Dana. I want to take her out on Sunday."

After a pause, Meg said, "All right. I understand

how much this means to your family. Are you taking her to visit your mother?''

"Mom can make her own visits, as she's informed me." He chuckled, remembering Grace's indignant remark that he needn't think breaking up with Meg had anything to do with her. "I want to show Dana the San Diego Zoo."

"She's awfully little. That's a great place but it might be overwhelming."

He hadn't visited the zoo in years. Still, what child didn't enjoy seeing monkeys and polar bears and giraffes? "We won't stay long. I know toddlers have a short attention span. Hey, I'm a pediatrician, remember?''

"Well…"

"Don't I deserve the same visiting privileges my mother does?" He was half-teasing, half-serious. Spending time with his daughter was partly a way to see Meg again, but he intended to remain an involved father, no matter what else happened.

"All right," she said.

"I'll pick her up at ten o'clock." Hugh calculated Mercy Canyon was located about an hour's drive from the zoo. They could eat lunch when they arrived and then, refreshed, enjoy the animals.

"She'll be ready." Meg sounded so wistful that Hugh had to stop himself from inviting her to join them. It was important that his meetings with Dana not be perceived as sneaky attempts to win Meg back.

The next day at work, he was assigned to analyze the case of a little boy who kept running away from home. Using the project's resources, he calculated what types of help might get to the root of the child's problem.

It buoyed him to realize what a positive impact he could have, with his medical skills and the new information he was gaining. Now all he had to do was figure out a way to solve his own problems.

"HE SEEMS TO BE accepting my decision," Meg told Judy on their break Thursday. It was midafternoon and even the regulars had abandoned the coffee shop. They sat in a rear booth where they could hear the door chimes if anyone came in.

"I can't believe Joe, or Hugh, or whatever his name is this week, would give up that easily." Judy adjusted a clip in her short blond hair.

Meg stared into the blackness of her coffee. She hadn't thought he would, either, she realized. At some level, she'd expected Hugh to decide that opening an office in town wasn't such a bad idea, after all.

"Men ought to think of someone other than themselves once in a while." Through the window, she watched her brother climb down from his truck cab, no doubt heading this way for a cup of coffee.

"Are you referring to Hugh or Tim?" Judy asked. "Sometimes it's hard to keep the players straight."

"My life is not a soap opera, even though it feels like one at the moment," Meg said. "I guess you remember that Tim refused to go to my father's birthday party. Now Dad's called the whole thing off. He's going to take Lynn to Las Vegas instead."

She heard the cafe's front door jangle open and knew it was Tim. Miguel could serve him coffee at the counter.

"That sounds like fun." Judy loved to go to the shows, eat at buffets and play the slot machines, although she always set herself strict betting limits when she and Sam went to Vegas.

"The point is to celebrate ten years on the wagon," Meg noted. "It isn't healthy for him to go to Vegas, with all that alcohol. Why subject himself to the temptation?"

"You can't blame your brother if your father does something self-destructive," Judy said.

"I guess not. But I wish Tim would let bygones be bygones." She drained her cup.

Masculine footsteps slapped against worn linoleum. Tim's gangly figure emerged in the back room. "Why didn't you tell me?" he demanded.

"About the party?" Meg asked, puzzled.

"What party?"

"Dad canceled his party because you're not coming."

"That's up to him," Tim said. "I'm talking about Hugh. I dropped by Mrs. Lincoln's trailer to give Dana a doll I bought her, and the first thing she said was, 'Mommy, Daddy fight.'"

"I don't know where she got that idea." Receiving a frown from Judy, Meg added, "Okay, we broke up, but we didn't *fight*. I told Dana that Daddy and I weren't friends anymore."

"Why not?" Tim sat down, his jaw thrust forward pugnaciously. "Did he mistreat you?"

"Of course not!" Meg said.

"I didn't think so. You know, sis, Joe is my friend, too," he said.

She didn't correct his use of the wrong name. "I know you guys got close."

"We just found him. I don't want to lose him again," Tim said. "He's like a, well, a big brother."

"He's a father figure," said Judy.

"Tim already has a father."

"No, I don't!" her brother flared. "Stop trying to foist Zack on me. There's no way to make up for what he did."

Meg wondered how she'd ended up fighting a battle on two fronts. She was irked with Tim about shunning their father, while he was blaming her for the breakup with Hugh.

"You have to let go of the past," she told her brother. "It would be a lot healthier than holding a grudge."

"What about you?" Tim demanded, his freckles standing out against his pale skin. "Aren't you holding on to the past, too?"

"In what way?" Meg demanded.

"You want Joe back," her brother said. "That's what you've wanted since the first moment you met Hugh. Well, if you love him, you'll accept him the way he is."

"And leave Mercy Canyon?" she said. "No one's asking you to give up your job or your home for Dad, only to be polite to him at his birthday party. Hugh's a different matter entirely."

"He's your husband."

"Not legally, he isn't."

"You promised to love, honor and cherish. I heard you!" Tim said.

The front door opened again, and voices chattered as a family came in. "End of discussion," she said. "If you want to be pals with Hugh, call him yourself."

"I will." Her brother stood up. "You can bet on it!"

As he stalked off, Meg pinched the bridge of her

nose to forestall an incipient headache. "I don't want to lose my brother."

"You won't." Judy patted her hand. "Tim loves you more than anybody."

Although she appreciated the sentiment, Meg was glad when her friend went to wait on the new arrivals. She had so many things to sort out in her head.

Why couldn't life remain on an even keel? Changes and quarrels unnerved her, bringing back wrenching memories of her childhood.

All she wanted was to stay where she belonged, surrounded by familiar faces. Not to fight with Tim. Not to lose Hugh.

He was coming on Sunday to see Dana. Feeling off-center after the confrontation with her brother, Meg wished now that she'd postponed the visit.

More voices from the front announced the arrival of additional customers. Shoving aside her worries, she rose and went to help them.

AFTER PUTTING IN a morning's work on Saturday, Hugh left Orange about noon. He'd promised to eat dinner with his family that night, and he wasn't looking forward to their questions about his situation with Meg.

Operating on instinct, he took a different freeway than usual and wound up in Redondo Beach. The closest parking space to Andrew's cottage was two blocks inland, but he didn't mind walking in the sea air.

Hugh wasn't sure why he'd come here, except that this was the one place where he and Meg had been truly happy since they reunited. It was after they made love that he'd begun to believe they could truly make a life together.

He missed her animated, sensitive face, the expressive amber eyes and her warm, welcoming mouth. It hurt too much even to think about her soft breasts and the pressure of her body against his.

Nothing was the same since last weekend. Even his excitement about his new job and the chance to help children couldn't compensate for his loss.

Yet how much should he sacrifice in order to keep her?

When Hugh reached the cottage, he was surprised to see the front door standing open. Andrew and Cindi weren't staying here, as far as he knew.

Concerned that something might be amiss, he approached the porch cautiously. From inside, the roar of a vacuum cleaner reassured him. Burglars didn't usually bother to clean the carpets when they broke into a house.

His brother employed a maid service, Hugh knew, and was about to stroll away when the noise cut off and a dark-haired woman came outside.

It was his sister-in-law.

They blinked at each other for a minute. "I wasn't expecting you," Cindi said. "Did Andrew loan you the cottage?"

He shook his head. "I needed to take a walk and this seemed like as good a place as any. Aren't you joining us for dinner tonight?"

"Yes. I just felt like cleaning." An embarrassed look came over Cindi's high-boned face. "That sounds stupid, doesn't it, when I don't need to."

"I guess some people consider it a form of therapy." Hugh strolled over to the porch.

"I can't clean at your mother's house. That's Hannah's domain." Cindi sank onto a glider seat. Hugh leaned against a railing across from her. "Usually, I don't need to do anything here, either. When you clean a place, though, it becomes more yours.''

''You decorated it and you own it. Of course it's yours.''

''It doesn't necessarily feel that way,'' she said.

In the fourteen years that his brother had been married, Hugh realized, he'd never before had such a private conversation with his sister-in-law. He had no idea how she felt about houses, or housework, or anything.

To him, she'd always been the efficient wife and mother on whom everyone depended. Only the shyness she'd shown around Meg indicated she wasn't as confident as she seemed.

''Is something wrong?'' He hoped she and his brother weren't having marital problems.

''With Andrew? No.'' Cindi twisted her hands together. ''Nothing is wrong, exactly.''

Hugh waited. One of the techniques he'd learned at his new job was for adults to remain silent and let young people talk. The same rule surely applied to other adults, too.

''I just talked to my mother on the phone,'' Cindi said at last. Her parents lived in San Francisco. Hugh had met them once, and came away with an impression of haughtiness.

''About what?'' he asked.

''My brother made partner in his law firm.'' She rocked the glider in agitation. ''He's being called a brilliant legal mind. My mother reminded me that I could have been in the same situation.''

Over the years, Hugh had almost forgotten that Cindi held a law degree. She'd quit work when she became pregnant the second time, with Angela. ''Being a wife and mother is every bit as important.''

"That's what I decided," she agreed. "I remember working those long hours and leaving William with a nanny. It broke my heart, and he was miserable. When the third nanny quit while I was pregnant, I knew I couldn't continue putting my children through the wringer."

"Does your brother have children?" Cindi rarely mentioned her family, Hugh realized.

"Yes. He also has a stay-at-home wife," she said. "He didn't have to make the choices I did. My parents don't care. I'm their daughter and they expected great things of me."

"So your mom was giving you a hard time." he said.

The glider creaked as she swung. "In her own subtle way, yes."

During his training that week, Hugh had learned a skill called "active listening," which meant trying to hear what was beneath the surface of the other person's words, and reflecting it back to that person for confirmation. Now he applied the lesson to his sister-in-law.

"Maybe the reason she bothers you so much is that you have mixed feelings about your decision," he said. "Do you think you're wasting your talents?"

Cindi studied him in dismay. "No! I mean..." She glared at the squeaky glider. "I'm going to oil this thing." Abruptly, she marched into the house and returned with a can of lubricant, which she applied.

Hugh waited. A minute later, the dark-haired woman resumed her seat. "Well?" he asked.

"Persistent, aren't you?"

"Some might call me stubborn," he agreed.

"Getting through law school was a huge amount of work and sacrifice," Cindi said. "I graduated with honors and made the law review, so I was primed for a big career.''

''It bothers you that you gave it up?''

''I don't want to be shut up all day and half the night practicing law.'' She rocked, soundlessly. ''Still, there are times when I wonder if I made the right choice.''

''Especially after talking to your mother,'' Hugh guessed.

Cindi laughed. ''Almost exclusively after talking to my mother,'' she said. ''Maybe I should work for a small law firm, handling routine wills and adoptions. Meg suggested...'' She stopped.

''You discussed this with Meg?'' He was torn between surprise and amusement. ''Mom said it was a short visit.''

''Short but meaningful,'' Cindi said. ''She's a terrific person.''

''You don't have to tell me.''

''Thanks for listening,'' she said. ''I hope you and Meg work things out. She's missing out on a great guy.''

''Thanks,'' he said. ''Maybe you could tell her that.''

''I wouldn't dare!''

A few minutes later, Cindi resumed her cleaning with a cheerful air and Hugh continued his walk. He had to admit that he was being inconsistent. He admired his sister-in-law for giving up her career, yet he couldn't imagine making a similar choice by leaving the Whole Child Project.

Were men and women that different? Or was it, as she'd said about her brother, that Hugh didn't have to make that choice because he could entrust his child's care to Meg?

Still, if he didn't move to Mercy Canyon as Meg wished, he would be choosing to let his daughter grow up in a fatherless household. Having a part-time dad wasn't the same as having one who lived with you.

How much of himself could he sacrifice for the sake of his family? Hugh wondered. And how would he feel later, if he made such a sacrifice?

Chapter Fifteen

On Sunday morning, Meg attended the early church service. Since they'd set their clocks back today for Pacific Standard Time, more people than usual were awake and in attendance.

Arriving home with a few minutes to spare, she changed from a dress into her usual jeans and shirt. Then, reluctant to let Hugh see her that way even though he would only be stopping in for a few minutes, she changed again, to a pair of navy slacks and a russet sweater.

It was embarrassing that she cared so much about his opinion, Meg thought. She nearly switched back into jeans, then decided that would be foolish.

In the front room, Dana was playing with blocks. Nearby on the coffee table lay a church flyer advertising a Halloween festival. It reminded Meg of something. "Sweetie, tell me what you want to be for Halloween. I need to make your costume."

"Punkin pie," her daughter said, looking up from a precarious pile she'd built.

"You want to be a pumpkin pie? Or you want to eat one?" Meg asked, amused.

"Me be punkin pie," the little girl repeated.

"That's what Abbie calls you, isn't it?" Meg remembered hearing her neighbor use the endearment. "I'm afraid I'm not that creative. How about a ballerina?"

"Princess," Dana said.

Meg nodded. "That I can handle."

At a knock, she wiped her suddenly damp hands on her slacks and went to answer. At the door stood Hugh, hands thrust in his pockets.

He raised an eyebrow questioningly, as if uncertain of his reception. A breeze ruffled his blond hair, giving him the air of an unruly boy.

"You need a haircut," Meg said.

"Do I?" He shook back the impromptu bangs. "I'll have to find a new barber in Orange."

She was on the point of telling him that Rosa could cut his hair, when she stopped herself. The point was to get on with her life, not try to take over his. "I packed a diaper bag. Dana's starting to potty train but you don't want to take any chances on a trip like this."

"I'll do whatever you think is best." Entering, he knelt and helped Dana straighten her tower. "That's a terrific job you're doing there, little one."

The baby threw her arms around his neck. "Daddy!" she said.

The sight of the pair so happy together sent a pang through Meg. She was the one who'd chosen for her and Hugh to go their separate ways.

If only he would come into her world instead of insisting that she give it up. If only he could be Joe, only with Hugh's greater confidence and knowledge.

"Do you think she might get cold?" Hugh asked, lifting his daughter.

"Here's her sweater." Meg removed it from the

couch and handed it over. "I'll help you put the child seat into your car."

"Great. I need to borrow your stroller, too." Hugh shot her a sideways glance as if about to suggest something more, then looked away. Had he meant to invite her along? If he had, Meg didn't think she could have resisted.

They went outside and loaded his car. Soon Dana was happily strapped into her seat with a bottle of milk and some toys to keep her busy.

"She might get fussy," Meg warned.

"I bought a couple of children's CDs to play en route," Hugh said. In the cool, clear morning light, his gaze swept her with sudden warmth. "We'll be fine."

Of course they'd be fine. Dana had always had a special bond with her father.

It was Meg who didn't feel fine. Although she left the toddler with her neighbor while she worked, she wasn't accustomed to being alone during her time off.

Meg knew she ought to look forward to reading, taking a hot bath or going to a movie. Instead, she found herself wishing she were heading for the zoo.

She forced herself to take a step backward. "I'll see you in a few hours."

"Around four o'clock." Hugh slid into the car. As he started it, he rolled down the window. "Hey, I've got an idea. I'll bet they have great animal costumes at the gift shop. We'll pick one out for Halloween."

With a wave, he put the car in gear and rolled away.

"No, wait!" Meg called. "She wants to be a..."

His sedan passed out of earshot, away through the trailer park. The word *princess* died in her throat.

A strong, irrational feeling rose in Meg that she

didn't want someone else picking her daughter's Halloween costume. Not even Hugh.

There was only one way to prevent it. Now that they were on the road, Meg would have to follow them. Fortunately, she had tonight off work.

Maybe she could catch Hugh's eye and pull him over en route. Otherwise, she'd have to drive to the zoo and find them there.

For some inexplicable reason, the prospect lifted her spirits.

DANA PROVED to be more of a trouper than Hugh had expected. After dozing during the drive to San Diego, she perked up on arrival at the zoo, fascinated by the people streaming in from the parking lot.

"You don't see crowds very often, do you?" Hugh asked his daughter as he pushed her stroller toward an admission booth.

"Pretty." She waved at a dark-skinned little girl wearing a bright pink dress.

An urge seized Hugh to take Dana shopping and buy her as many pretty dresses as she wanted. Although there was nothing wrong with her light blue frock embroidered with daisies, it would be fun to spoil her.

Meg might not like it, though, he reminded himself, and stayed on course.

Inside the park, he found a restaurant and searched the menu for toddler-appropriate foods. As a pediatrician, he knew she should eat a balanced diet with plenty of fruits and vegetables.

As a father at the zoo, however, he had to make do with what was available. He settled for a small hamburger, which he cut into pieces, plus French fries and milk.

For himself, he chose the same. Dana laughed at seeing her father eat the identical food and, to humor her, Hugh cut up his hamburger, too.

Afterward, they washed their hands and went for a ride on the aerial tramway. For the next hour and a half, Hugh alternated child-centered activities like the petting zoo with visits to the park's unique facilities. These included the giant panda research station and a rain forest where they were able to view hippos swimming via large underwater windows.

When Dana gave a big yawn, he steered her back to the entrance and into the gift shop. Other visitors, including a group of Japanese tourists, wandered in delight through the large store.

"What would you like for a souvenir?" Hugh asked. "How about a stuffed panda?"

As he reached for the stuffed animal, he glimpsed a curvy red-haired woman who reminded him, heartstoppingly, of Meg. When he turned to get a better look, however, she had vanished.

"Runaway imagination," he muttered.

"Hippo!" Ignoring the panda, Dana pointed to a large plastic hippopotamus.

Hugh handed it to her. "That doesn't look very cuddly."

"Swim!" She raised the toy triumphantly.

"I don't think it's a bath toy." When he tried to pry it gently away, Dana clung fast.

"Mine," she said. "Love hippo."

He shrugged and put away the panda. "It won't keep you warm at night, sweetheart, but you can have it if you want it."

The Japanese tourists, summoned by their guide, cleared out of the gift shop. As it emptied, Hugh caught sight of the woman he'd seen before, standing with her back to him examining some hand puppets.

Darned if that riotous, short mane didn't look exactly like Meg's. Hadn't she also been wearing navy slacks today?

"Book." Dana pointed to a rack of colorful children's volumes.

"That's a good idea. I'm sure your mother would approve." Glad to be distracted from his ridiculous preoccupation with a strange woman, Hugh knelt and selected a couple of picture books. "Which one do you like?"

Her expression solemn, Dana examined her choices. "This," she announced, displaying one with an intimidating gorilla on the cover.

"Did I pick that?" Hugh had tried to stick to cute, cuddly animals. He'd obviously scooped up an extra book in the process.

"King Kong," said his daughter. "Friend."

She must have watched a movie or animated cartoon about the movie character. Hugh hoped the creature wouldn't give her nightmares. "Are you sure?"

Dana nodded and hugged the book, along with the hippo.

As he adjusted the diaper bag on his shoulder, Hugh remembered that he'd promised to buy a costume. Along with a book and a toy, that might be considered overdoing it, but he'd missed the last two birthdays and Christmases.

"Okay, let's see what—" He stopped. Staring back at him from the costume rack was the woman he'd seen before. She was, unquestionably, Meg.

"She wants to be a princess," she said.

"Excuse me?"

"You didn't give me a chance to tell you," she said.

"You followed us to the San Diego Zoo just to tell me that? Although I am glad to see you," he amended.

"It seemed important at the time," Meg admitted with a rueful grin. "The only problem was, after I got here, I couldn't find you. So I staked out the gift shop."

"I'm glad you did," Hugh said. "Our daughter has developed a fascination with hippos and gorillas. I want a second opinion."

"She has her own ideas about things, doesn't she?" Meg crouched by her daughter to examine the book and the toy hippo.

"I like these," said Dana.

"They're fine. Not what I'd choose, but she's the one who's going to play with them." Rising, Meg took a deep breath. "Maybe the costume was sort of an excuse. I guess I was uncomfortable at having her whisked away to a strange place without me."

"We should be doing things together." Hugh knew at once, from the way her back stiffened, that he'd said the wrong thing.

"Let's pick her costume, shall we?" Meg replied, and indicated the rack.

There was no point in arguing, so he pushed the stroller over and stood by while Meg displayed one costume after another to her daughter. Each was cuter than the next: a panda, a monkey, a polar bear, a parrot.

Dana laughed and clapped. She didn't seem to care which one was chosen.

"What do you think of this?" Meg set a duck's cap on Dana's head. The bill of the cap served as the bird's bill, and its eyes peered at them myopically from atop her crown.

Staring at herself in a nearby mirror, Dana nodded happily. "Mine!" she said.

Her mother stroked the body of the costume, which sprang with little wings. "It's adorable." Tears came to her eyes.

Hugh felt a little sentimental about selecting a costume, too, but he couldn't help wondering if this meant something more to Meg. "What's going on?"

She shrugged. "I was remembering...oh, it's silly."

"Tell me," Hugh said.

At the front of the shop, a group of German-speaking tourists came inside and began examining the merchandise. He was glad the two of them stood in a secluded corner where they could chat undisturbed.

"When I was eight, I was in a foster home at Halloween," Meg said. "The foster mom made her own daughter a wonderful dragon costume. I'd never seen anything so fancy."

"What about you?" he asked.

"She let me choose from among her daughter's old costumes. They were nice but they hadn't been made especially for me. The love was missing." In Meg's drooping shoulders, Hugh saw that she still suffered the pain of nearly twenty years ago.

"Did your brother have the same reaction?" He rocked Dana's stroller to keep her pacified.

"Tim was happy with the costume he picked," she said. "Of course, he was really little then."

"He didn't mind the foster homes as much as you did?" Hugh asked.

She took a minute to consider. "At the time, I didn't think he did. But he's the one who can't forgive Dad. He won't even go to his birthday party next month, so Dad canceled it."

"You sound upset," Hugh observed.

"Not for my sake! For Dad's." She frowned, deep in thought. "I tried to be all things to my brother. I guess I failed."

Hugh was surprised at such a negative comment. "You took care of him."

"Even so, he's got this anger inside, against Dad." Meg blinked back a tear. "He wouldn't be angry if I'd done enough."

Hugh curved one arm around her. "You demand too much of yourself."

She rested her head on his shoulder. "I don't want much, really. A happy family. Safety. For Dana and Tim to know where home is."

"It's with you," Hugh said.

She sucked in a shaky breath. "That's right."

"I want to make my home with you, too," he said.

Suddenly reacting to his nearness, Meg moved away. "I'm sorry. I didn't mean to blubber all over you." She wiped her eyes with a tissue.

"It's a funny thing," Hugh said. "When I lost my past, my life veered onto an unpredictable course. Your past, on the other hand, won't let you go."

"I wouldn't want to lose my memories, even the painful ones," Meg said. "They're part of who I am."

In the stroller, Dana began to fidget. "Go potty," she said.

"I'll take her." Meg collected the little girl. "I don't think she belongs in the men's room."

"Dads are liberated these days," Hugh replied. He wasn't sure how much he believed it, though.

Besides, he had to pay for the duck costume, the book and the hippo.

MEG LET HUGH take Dana home in his car while she followed. She couldn't blame him for wanting to enjoy his father-daughter outing to the last drop.

Besides, it was good to have time alone. The strong emotions awakened by their conversation still squeezed inside her chest.

Every time she thought the old wounds had healed, they caught her off guard with their power. Yet she felt better for having shared them with Hugh.

She'd never opened up to a man this way before, not even Joe. There was something reassuring about talking to Hugh.

Dana was asleep by the time they arrived at the mobile home park. She didn't awaken even when Hugh carried her inside to her crib.

"She's good for a couple of hours," Meg said as they stood gazing down at their daughter.

"We could send out for pizza." Hugh stood close, one arm almost touching her as he gripped the crib rail.

Meg wanted him to stay. All evening, all night, forever. To share a quiet, cozy future where they could hold on to each other.

Maybe it was possible. In any case, they didn't have to resolve the future right now. With a nod, she led him out of the room and closed the door behind them.

"Does Hugh Menton like mushrooms, or is he a pepperoni guy?" She decided not to mention Joe's preference, curious to see what he would choose.

"I have this craving for tomatoes and black olives," he said. "What do you think?"

"Joe usually ordered sausage," she admitted.

"I'll bet Joe didn't know much about cholesterol." Hugh took out his cell phone. "What's the closest pizza delivery place?"

They ordered, and played dominoes until the pizza came. Then they watched a trivia game show while they ate. Hugh knew a lot of the answers, just as Joe used to.

After they finished, they cleared away the remains of the meal. In the kitchen, standing by the counter, Hugh kissed Meg, and she ran her hands lovingly across his shoulders.

Tonight, the differences between them seemed to drop away. She didn't want to question the change too closely. She needed him too much.

He caught her derriere and held her against him, swaying in a rhythm that stirred wild drumbeats inside her. She melted into him, wordlessly yearning.

They fitted so perfectly together that Meg could hardly believe they were still wearing clothes. With a sense of relief, she lifted off her sweater and leaned back as Hugh lowered her bra and cupped her breasts possessively.

"Mine. Entirely mine." He kissed her again.

They left a trail of clothes on their way to the bedroom. Meg caressed him all over and felt his muscles tighten in her hands.

His sculpted, golden body was splendid in the nude. Lingering sunrays penetrating her blinds sparked his eyes with green fire as he eased her across the sheets.

When he bent to mouth her nipples, Meg gasped in sheer pleasure. She had no defenses against him and wanted none.

There was a moment's inexplicable regret when Hugh found protection in her drawer left over from their married days and put it on. She felt a longing for their union to plant the miracle of life inside her again.

Meg's thoughts rippled away like water. Holding himself above her, smiling with shared delight, Hugh gazed deep into her eyes and entered her with infinite care.

Meg cried out and clutched his taut bottom. They rocked together, his chest brushing her breasts, his power thrusting in and out of her. Sheer sensation blotted out conscious thought until the two of them soared together into a blissful white light.

Meg yearned for this joy to last forever. Then waves of rapture rolled over her, blotting out everything else.

In this perfect moment, there was neither past nor future. Only completion.

HUGH'S BODY reverberated with satisfaction long after the excitement ebbed. He lay cradling Meg, not wanting to leave, yet knowing he had to be at work early.

Finally, reluctantly, he eased away. "I've got to go."

"No." She caught his wrist. "This is your place. Here."

"I wish…" …*that there was a solution so we could both get what we want.* "I wish I could stay," he finished and, giving her a kiss, went to clean up.

When he was dressed, he came back and sat on the edge of the bed. "I'd like to spend Halloween with you." That was next Wednesday.

"We'll be going trick or treating around six," she said sleepily. "I arranged to work a morning shift that day."

Arriving by six meant fighting rush-hour traffic. It would be worth it. "I'll do my best to be on time."

He wanted to point out that tonight demonstrated how much the two of them belonged together. It wouldn't help to pressure her, though, and he couldn't stay to debate the matter.

Tomorrow, for the first time, he would be seeing clients—needy children—for the Whole Child Project. He didn't want to risk being late.

Baby Bonus?

William Baird's property belonged to me, and he would pay to claim his daughter.

"I assume . . . for the time, at least, he can be here . . . ."

. . . clear to Meg . . . . What . . . . only meant to help . . . .

Chapter Sixteen

From Monday morning to Wednesday evening was only two and a half days. To Meg, it felt like an eternity. Without Hugh, her bed was cold and empty. Even playing with Dana in the evenings wasn't the same without him.

It was a relief on Tuesday night when Tim dropped by. Meg and her brother hadn't exactly parted on the warmest of terms last week after discussing their father.

As usual, he walked directly to the refrigerator. "You need more beer," he said after looking inside.

"Buy your own," she returned. "I hardly ever drink the stuff." She didn't want to encourage her brother's alcohol consumption, even though he'd never showed signs of overindulging.

Tim returned to the living room munching a slice of leftover pizza. "Who ordered tomatoes and olives? This is sissy stuff."

"Tell it to Hugh," Meg retorted. Immediately, she wished she'd kept silent.

"You're back together!" he whooped.

"He came to see Dana," she corrected.

"Dana's too little to eat pizza." Tim draped himself over a corner of the couch.

"Okay, we ate dinner together. We're…friends." Nothing fundamental had changed, after all. As far as Meg knew, Hugh still had no intention of moving to Mercy Canyon.

She wished she could make him understand how much her home meant to her. Being surrounded by familiar people and places was a constant reassurance after the disruptions of her childhood.

"I've been thinking about Dad," Tim said.

Optimism stirred inside Meg. Maybe her brother was ready to forgive.

"And it makes me angry," he went on, dashing her hopes. "Why did he have to cancel his birthday party just because I won't be there? He hasn't seen me in years, so what's the difference?"

Meg might have stamped her foot in frustration if she hadn't been sitting on the floor, holding Dana in her lap. "You mean a lot to him."

"He's trying to manipulate me by hurting you," Tim said. "One thing I've learned about boozers—don't correct me, that's what I call them—is that they twist things around to their own advantage. The guys at work who continually show up late and miss assignments give one excuse after another. It's always somebody else's fault. They never admit they were drunk."

Meg struggled to be fair. After Joe's disappearance, she and her father had spent a lot of time together and he'd been honest about his past.

"Dad admits he used to be self-centered," she said. "He told himself it was Mom's fault for insisting on marriage and children when he wasn't ready. That we weren't really his responsibility."

"See?" Tim wiped his hand on a paper napkin. "Can I have the last slice?"

"Go ahead."

When he came out of the kitchen, he said, "Just because Dad admits his past sins doesn't mean he isn't taking advantage of the situation now. He wants to pretend we're a loving family. I refuse to be a hypocrite."

Meg had seen the hurt in her father's eyes as he watched the door at Lynn's exhibit, waiting for a glimpse of his son. "You don't have to pretend anything you don't feel. Just show up."

"He had his chance to be my father when I needed him. When you needed him, too," Tim said. "It's too late. I'm not his son anymore."

Meg tried in vain to swallow the lump in her throat. "I did everything I could for you. Why are you so angry?"

"This isn't about you!" Tim said. "Come on, sis, let's not fight. Let's watch *Buffy the Vampire Slayer*."

Meg took Dana to bed, then rejoined her brother. The problem, she thought as they sat in front of the TV, was that while she had Hugh and Dana and Tim and Dad and her close friends in Mercy Canyon, she couldn't get them all together. One person or another was always just out of reach.

She wanted the perfect life she'd longed for as a child. She wanted everything wrapped in a shiny package, tied up with a big red bow.

Was that too much to ask?

ON WEDNESDAY afternoon, Hugh's last patient appointment was canceled unexpectedly, and a social worker called to postpone their four o'clock meeting until the following week.

He found himself free at three-thirty. Plenty of time

to drive to Mercy Canyon, but there was something he had to do first.

From the clinic, Hugh drove to a specialty Halloween store that had sprung up in a formerly vacant storefront. Costumes were marked down half price today, so he went whole hog in buying supplies.

He took them to the address of a patient he'd seen earlier that day for a routine checkup. Sandra lived in a foster home in Tustin, a slightly shabby ranch-style house with a patchy lawn and several young children riding tricycles in the fenced yard.

She might, he suspected, be suffering from the beginnings of anorexia. He wanted to keep a close eye on her and help build her self-esteem at the same time.

Still in his white coat, Hugh rang the doorbell. Paying home visits to patients, almost unthinkable for a regular pediatrician, was appropriate in the Whole Child Project. While he didn't want to interfere excessively, it was important to let the children know that they mattered as individuals.

Sandra herself answered the door. A thin fourteen-year-old with tangled hair, she had dark, wary eyes. "Yes? Oh, Dr. Menton! Did I do something wrong?"

How typical, he thought with a twist of sympathy, that her first reaction was to fear being in trouble. The girl had a history of running away from her neglectful parents and of skipping school. "No, of course not. I brought you something."

Suddenly shy, Sandra mumbled as she invited him inside. Hugh stepped into a cluttered but clean living room. "My foster mom is taking a nap," the girl said.

"No need to wake her." He reached into his shopping bag. "You said you wanted to be a witch for Halloween."

She shrugged. "It was just an idea. I'm too old for trick or treating."

"Aren't you escorting the younger children?"

"Well, yeah, but..."

He pulled out the wig. "You'll need this."

Her mouth curved, breaking the solemnity of her expression. "It's for me? I mean, I guess it was left over from something, right?"

"I bought it for you." He took out a makeup kit, plastic fangs and a dark blue spangled robe. "The whole ensemble. Do you like it?"

"Wow!" She held the robe against her thin frame. "I didn't know you could find stuff like this at a thrift shop."

"I didn't. I got it at the Halloween store." Hugh retrieved the last item. "Now this splendid item is a collapsible broom." He unfolded the hinged handle. "Not much good in a high wind but it should provide reliable transportation otherwise."

Puzzled, Sandra examined the stylized broom. Slowly, a smile warmed her face. "You're joking."

"That's right," he said. "Brooms aren't all that reliable. They only fly on Halloween."

Sandra laughed, looking younger and more carefree than before. Hugh was glad to see the change.

"You didn't really buy these for me, did you?" she asked. "That's a joke, too, right?"

"Not at all," he said. "You're a good kid. I know you help take care of the younger children around here, and you deserve a treat yourself."

"Maybe I'll go to my girlfriend's party later," she said. "I wasn't going to because I didn't have a costume."

"Have fun." Hugh was tempted to add a parental

pep talk about how she was as good as anyone else. Last week's training, however, had taught him that at-risk kids were turned off by lectures. "I hope I'm not undermining your homework time."

"I'll get it done right now," Sandra said, turning the wig over in her hands as if she could hardly believe it was real. "I can't wait to try this on."

"If you can get someone to take a photograph, I'd love to see it on your next visit." Because of his suspicions about anorexia, Hugh had scheduled her to return in a few weeks.

"Okay!" With a little skip, she hurried off into the house. Hugh went out, sidestepping scattered toys on the walkway.

He glanced at his watch. It was after five, and he had a long drive to make. But the detour had been worth it.

AT FIRST, Meg was annoyed when Hugh arrived twenty minutes late. When he told her the reason, however, her irritation vanished.

"Sandra sounds like me when I was a kid," she said. "I'm so glad you could help her."

"I've barely scratched the surface," Hugh replied as they pushed Dana's stroller to a nearby trailer illuminated with holiday lights. "She needs a lot of guidance and encouragement."

"Even a small gesture means a lot, coming from an important person like a doctor." Meg lifted her daughter and carried her to the door, passing a small group of departing goblins, ghosts and superheroes.

"Twick tweat!" Dana said loudly to the screen door.

In the opening appeared Abbie Lincoln, who dropped a candy bar into Dana's plastic bag. "Isn't she precious?'' She glanced into the darkness to where Hugh stood waiting. "Good to see you, Joe!''

"It's good to be here,'' he said.

They made the rounds of the other trailers, where people clucked delightedly over Dana in her duck costume. Then the three of them drove to Meg's church, where Dana threw balls at a hoop, played games and won a plate of brownies in a cakewalk.

Meg sighed as a group of junior high students ran by. "I used to baby-sit some of those kids when I was in high school,'' she said. "I can't believe how they've grown.''

Quite a few people stopped her to welcome Hugh back. Although Meg had told everyone the circumstances, they still called him Joe. He didn't seem to mind.

She could almost imagine, for this short space of time, that they were a happily married couple with their future secure.

ALTHOUGH HUGH had always had friends and relatives around as he grew up, they hadn't formed a community like this. Meg seemed to know everyone, and they clearly had a special place for her in their hearts.

Maybe it was selfish of him to want to take her away. He'd thought that when she talked about Mercy Canyon, she was referring only to her brother and a small group of friends, all of whom could easily visit her elsewhere.

He'd believed that he was meeting her halfway and trying to work things out. Instead, what he'd done was demand that she change her life to suit him.

His ambitions and need to make good use of his

talents would always be important. However, his marriage was vital to his happiness.

Maybe some compromise was possible. He needed to sort out his impressions before he said anything to Meg, though.

At nine o'clock, Hugh took her and their sleepy daughter back to the trailer. He drove with extra care because of the young costumed revelers prowling the streets.

He could picture Dana growing up as part of the happy throng. Perhaps there would be more children, too, another daughter or a son.

Hugh's breath caught as a longing swept over him to watch his child mature from an infant into a toddler. He'd missed that stage with Dana. He didn't want to miss anything more.

"Would you like to come in?" Meg stood in the doorway, holding Dana against her shoulder.

"I'd better not." Although the hour was early, he needed to think. "I'm sure we've both got a long day tomorrow."

"Are you planning to take Dana out next weekend?" Meg asked.

"I may have to work." Hugh wasn't sure why he said that, since he hadn't been scheduled at the clinic. Because of a germ of an idea rattling around the back of his mind, perhaps. One he couldn't put his finger on yet.

Meg lifted her chin, perhaps to hide the disappointment. "Let me know when you want to see her."

"I'll do that." He gave her a friendly nod and left.

Okay, Hugh, you acted like a big jerk back there, he told himself as he got in his car. Meg had practically invited him into her arms, and had paved the way for them to get together on the weekend. Both times he'd said no.

Why?

He didn't understand himself, Hugh mused as he rolled the car toward the park exit. Some notion was struggling to drag itself out of the muck in his brain, but he couldn't get a hold on it.

On the main street, he drove until the Back Door Cafe appeared ahead on his left. Impulsively, he stopped in front.

A paper Casper the Ghost dangled inside the door as he entered, and black and orange crepe paper stretched across one wall. He'd forgotten that Judy liked to tack up ornaments for holidays. They were sparse, though. She would have to combine her decorations for all the holidays to really fill up the place.

It would be a designer's nightmare. On the other hand, such a crazy quilt might be a lot of fun.

Seated at the counter, Tim raised his cup of coffee in salute. "I'm about to make a run to Sacramento with the truck. I'm fortifying myself."

Hugh took the stool next to him. "When will you be back?"

"Saturday," Tim said. "Why?"

"I'm not sure," he admitted. "I have a vague idea about Meg."

"Don't try to talk me into attending Dad's birthday party," Tim warned.

With his red hair and freckles, the young man resembled an overgrown adolescent. Hugh knew better than to treat him as one, though.

"It's none of my business," he said. "When was the party supposed to be, anyway? This coming weekend?"

"No, the next one." Tim signaled to Miguel, who refilled his cup. Through the opening to the kitchen, Sam gave Hugh a wave, which he returned.

"You wouldn't happen to have your father's phone number, would you?" Hugh asked. "I might need to get in touch with him."

"Meg has it."

"Without telling her," he added.

"Oh?" Tim's eyebrows rose in curiosity. "I might have it." From his pocket, he produced an electronic organizer. After few taps of the button, he displayed the number on the small screen.

As Hugh copied it, the idea swirling through his consciousness took shape. "Listen, I have this plan but I need to run it by a few people. Including you."

"Yeah?"

Catching Sam's attention, he signaled to his friend to join them. "We'd have to pull it together quickly or Meg will get wind of it. Possibly by Saturday."

"Pull what together?" asked Judy, approaching from the back room.

"A wedding," Hugh said.

HAD SHE MISREAD Hugh, or was he reluctant to spend time with her? Meg wondered as she drove to work on Thursday.

Maybe, after giving it some thought, he'd decided she was right. That they belonged in different worlds.

Her heart plunged. *I didn't really mean it. No, no, I did mean it, but I wanted him to love me so much that he would change his plans and move to Mercy Canyon.*

There seemed little likelihood of that now. She had to admit, based on the anecdote about the girl and the witch costume, that she understood why he cared so much about this new project. It was certainly more challenging than handling routine sore throats and ear infections in a small office.

If only there'd been someone like Hugh to give her hope when she was a foster child, it would have meant so much. She hated to deny other kids that chance by persuading him to leave the project.

Yet she had her own needs to consider. Last night, seeing so many friends at the carnival and in her park, had reaffirmed how much she loved this community.

Troubled, Meg parked her car in one of the employee slots behind the coffee shop and went inside. At midafternoon, the place was dead, so she set herself to refilling condiment dispensers and giving the tables an extra cleaning.

She was brewing fresh coffee when Sam stuck his head out of the kitchen. "Did you notice the schedule change?"

"No. What change?" Wiping her hands on her apron, Meg walked through the swinging doors and examined the staff schedule posted on a bulletin board.

Her shift on Friday had been given to the new waitress who'd been filling in. On Saturday, Meg didn't come on duty until five.

"What's going on?" she asked. "I need those hours, Sam."

"A person wouldn't know it, the way you've been taking time off," he said.

She glared at him. "You and Judy encouraged me! I thought you wanted Hugh and me to spend time together."

Sam shrugged with uncharacteristic indifference. "All the same, I've got a restaurant to run. That new waitress has been very accommodating, and she needs the extra hours.''

"But…'' Meg cut off her protest. When her boss got this mulish expression on his face, there was no point in arguing.

Judy bustled past. "Did Sam tell you we're not bowling on Saturday? Rosa's been hired to fix hair for a big party.''

"Oh.'' Meg had a disoriented sensation. She counted on her orderly routine, more, perhaps, than she'd realized. "Are you guys mad at me or something?''

"It's nothing personal,'' Sam said, and went back to preparing food.

From time to time that evening, Meg tried to puzzle out a hidden meaning behind the change. Did her friends feel jealous of the time she'd spent with Hugh? Or perhaps Sam really was annoyed about her taking time off during the last few weeks.

He stayed in the kitchen, giving her no chance to sound him out. Judy seemed unusually absorbed in her customers. Even Miguel wasn't quite himself, replenishing the coffee carafes more often than necessary and avoiding the usual wisecracks during lulls in business.

Maybe it was her imagination, Meg told herself. Or her unhappiness about losing a shift might show in her own behavior, making her colleagues feel constrained around her.

On Friday, it turned out to be a good thing that she wasn't working. Abbie's younger daughter went into labor while her husband was out of town, which meant Abbie needed to be with her instead of baby-sitting.

Along with Dana, Meg watched Abbie's grandchildren for the day. The six children kept her running like crazy around the trailer park's small playground, and she couldn't get them all to nap at once in her two-bedroom unit.

She didn't mind, though. The children distracted her from the irrational worries aroused by her disrupted schedule.

It was amazing how many scenarios Meg could come up with to distress herself. Just a minor change in her routine brought up all sorts of concerns about the future. After all, if she couldn't rely on Sam to act in predictable ways, she couldn't take anything for granted.

What if Abbie had to stop baby-sitting permanently and Meg couldn't find a replacement? What if Sam and Judy decided to sell the coffee shop and indulge their lifelong dream of moving to Alaska?

Even though none of these things was likely to happen, Meg felt the ground trembling beneath her feet. She'd experienced the same insecurity as a child when neither of her parents was there for her.

Sternly, she reined in her imaginings. In any case, she could cope with whatever came.

On Saturday morning, Tim was scheduled to return from a run to Sacramento. When he didn't show up at her place, Meg called him.

"I was expecting to see you," she said. "I bought more beer." She'd picked it up at the store despite her hesitation. After all, she did want her brother to feel welcome at her trailer.

"It's kind of early in the morning for beer, sis," he muttered into the phone.

"There's coffee. And I brought home doughnuts." Usually she didn't have to invite him over once, let alone twice.

After a moment's silence, her brother said, "I've got plans this morning. Maybe I'll see you tomorrow."

"Sure." Meg hung up. She wished she knew what was wrong with him, and with everybody.

Or, maybe, what was wrong with her.

"HAVE YOU CONSIDERED that this idea might backfire?" Gazing into the hall mirror, Grace put the finishing touches on her upsweep of gray hair.

"Oh, Grandma, I think it's romantic!" Angela twirled in the deep rose party dress she'd bought for a sixth grade dance.

William fidgeted inside his Sunday suit, while Cindi looked lovely in a lavender cocktail dress. She had decided not to go back to work until her children were older, and seemed happy with the decision.

"It's a bit high-handed," Hugh admitted, standing in the hallway of his mother's home, "but it's the best I could come up with."

He'd driven to the Hollywood Hills today to collect his tuxedo, and to accompany his family as they ventured outside their usual territory. He was impressed with their willingness to go along with his scheme, even Andrew, who also wore a tuxedo.

His trip here had meant leaving the last-minute details in Sam and Judy's hands. Hugh was more grateful than ever for their support.

"Surprises can be fine," Andrew said. "Like the one you sprang on me. I'm glad you arranged for Barry to join me, although it wouldn't have hurt to let me know you'd contacted him. I'd have liked to arrange for him to come sooner than next March."

"Aren't things working out with Dr. Withers?" The retired doctor was filling in three days a week.

"Dr. Dithers is more like it," Andrew said. "The patients love him, but the pharmacies can't read his handwriting and he isn't up on the latest medical advances. I have to double-check all his reports and recommendations."

"Who cares about that stuff? We're going to a wedding!" chirped Angela.

"It's not a real wedding," William said. "They'd have to get a license and a clergyman for that."

"It's a real wedding," Hugh said. "Just not the kind you're thinking of."

"What do you mean, Uncle Hugh?" Angela asked.

"You'll see," he said. "Time to go."

All of a sudden, he felt nervous. What if his plan did backfire?

Well, at least with his family and friends all personally witnessing the calamity, he wouldn't have to worry about explaining it to anyone.

BY SATURDAY afternoon, Abbie had returned bubbling with happy news about her new granddaughter. Meg was glad everything had turned out well and grateful that her neighbor could take care of Dana for the evening.

When she arrived outside the coffee shop, Meg was surprised to see a cluster of cars filling the lot this early in the evening. There was quite a range of vehicles, including several expensive ones.

She remembered that Rosa was fixing ladies' hair for a party. That didn't explain why she spotted her brother's car, and, a moment later, Hugh's. They certainly weren't getting *their* hair done at the salon.

A hand-lettered sign on the glass door of the coffee

shop read Closed For Private Party. Sam hadn't mentioned anything about that.

Meg was so curious she nearly stopped and entered through the front. Sam insisted that his staff park in back, though, and she didn't want to get on his bad side. It might give him a reason to take away more of her hours.

Swinging around the shopping center, Meg halted in her usual spot. As she killed the motor, she could hear her heart hammering. Whatever was going on, it must involve her. That was the only possible explanation for Hugh's presence.

When Meg was young, unexpected turns of events had never been pleasant. Usually they meant another stay in a foster home.

No one could send her to a strange place now, she reminded herself. She was in charge of her life.

Except that she couldn't control how much she loved Hugh. As she got out of the car, Meg wished urgently that he was at her side to reassure her.

Last Sunday when they'd made love again, she'd discovered how much she needed him. She was just as vulnerable as she'd been as a child, because losing him would tear her world apart.

She wished she'd never tried to drive him away. Most of all, she hoped he hadn't come to say goodbye.

Clutching her purse, Meg straightened her spine and marched toward the restaurant.

Chapter Seventeen

While she washed her hands in the employees' rest room, Meg listened to the murmur of voices and a jumble of music through the wall. It sounded like a lot of people had arrived.

She tightened the apron around her gray skirt and blouse. No matter how hard she tried, she couldn't come up with an explanation that made sense. She would have to walk into it unprepared.

Emerging in a short hallway that led past the kitchen, Meg noticed a piñata hanging straight ahead. Was this a birthday celebration?

She emerged in the back dining room and halted, trying to make sense of what she saw.

Judy had gone crazy with the decorations. One corner of the room was done up for Halloween, another corner for Thanksgiving. Someone had erected a Christmas tree in the middle and draped artificial holly over the broad arch that connected the front and rear dining areas.

And the people! Rosa and Ramon, dancing to salsa music from a boom box, wore their colorful *Cinco de Mayo* finery. Good heavens, there were Lynn and her father gyrating alongside them, Lynn in an artist's smock and Zack in a polo shirt bearing the logo of the shoe store he managed.

Feeling as if she'd dropped into an alternate universe, Meg walked under the holly.

In the front room, ''We've Only Just Begun'' played on a second boom box. Her gaze swept a booth decorated as a wedding bower with white lace and a huge spray of pink roses in a vase. The booth behind it was draped with red-white-and-blue Fourth of July bunting.

Mostly what she noticed, though, was Hugh, stunning in his tuxedo and wearing an even more appealing smile. Dazed, Meg recognized his mother, brother and sister-in-law, all dressed up. They looked like they were going to a wedding, but whose?

Out of the kitchen came Sam and Judy, wearing their bowling T-shirts. Tim, looking macho in his trucker's jacket, danced with a tall woman in a business suit whom Meg identified as Dr. Archikova.

Surreptitiously, she pinched herself, a corny but effective way to make sure she wasn't dreaming. It hurt.

''What's going on?'' she asked.

''We're celebrating a marriage.'' Stepping forward, Hugh caught her hands in his.

''Who's tying the knot?'' On the counter behind him, Meg spotted the strangest wedding cake she'd ever seen. Each tier was a different color.

''It's the marriage of two worlds,'' Hugh said. ''Yours and mine. For all the seasons of our lives.''

She didn't trust herself to speak because she might burst into tears. Or laughter. Everyone stared at her, awaiting a reaction, and the silence lengthened.

''I told you she might not like it,'' Grace warned her son. ''He means well,'' she added, to Meg.

''Sorry about cutting your hours yesterday and today," Sam said. "We needed time to set this thing up."

"You cut my hours to set up this party?" Meg turned to Hugh. "You didn't have to go to all this trouble. You could have just talked to me."

His green eyes sparkled. "Sometimes words aren't enough. I wanted to show you how much everyone cares. So you'd understand that we can bring our families and our communities together."

When the song ended, Tim turned off the boom box. "Hugh's very persuasive. He got me and Dad into the same room, for your sake," he said.

Zack appeared beneath the holly. "It was good of you to come," he told his son. "At least we agree on doing what's best for your sister."

Tim addressed Meg. "I didn't mean to hurt you. I never realized how much you took my behavior to heart, until Hugh pointed it out. It was selfish, hanging on to my resentment toward Dad when you'd sacrificed so much to give me a decent childhood. That's why I've agreed to go to his birthday party."

"Thank you!" Meg said.

"It's next weekend," Lynn said, standing beside Zack. "I hope you and Hugh can make it, too."

"Are you kidding?" Tim said. "They'll break a leg getting there."

He didn't look directly at his father, however, let alone embrace the man. Meg knew better than to ask for miracles.

"I'm still a bit confused," she admitted. "What's all this mean?"

"That we can meet each other halfway," Hugh said. "For example, we can live here in Mercy Canyon. Rent an apartment or buy a house. I'll commute."

"You would do that?" Meg hadn't expected him to take on a drive that could run an hour or longer each way during rush hour.

"If it means keeping you as my wife, I'd commute a lot farther than this," Hugh said.

Gazing into his loving eyes, she realized that for once she wasn't looking for traces of Joe. The spontaneous, down-to-earth man she'd fallen in love with and married was there, of course, and so was the intellectual doctor who'd replaced him. She loved them both.

Her heart felt as big as a bowling ball. Not heavy, though. Light enough to float her right up to the ceiling.

"I wanted happiness locked in a bank vault." Slowly, Meg surveyed the people around her. "Safe and predictable and never changing. But I would have missed so much."

If her life hadn't changed, she'd never have known Andrew and Cindi, who were beaming as if they'd never had a moment's doubt about her. Or Grace, who formed a picture of quiet contentment as she rested her arms around Angela and William. Not to mention Dr. Archikova, who was a good sport for coming tonight.

"Thank you, everyone," Meg went on. "Thanks for going to so much trouble. Thanks for coming tonight, too."

"We're not done yet," Hugh said. "Tim, cue the music, would you?"

Her brother pressed a button on the boom box, releasing the soothing tones of a Mozart air. It made an odd contrast to the salsa music drifting from the back.

"As I said, this is a meeting of worlds." Hugh dropped onto one knee on the floor. "I sure hope the proprietors keep this place clean,'' he added with a grin.

"You want me to toss you a cleaning rag while you're down there?" Sam asked.

"Later," he responded. "Hey, Andrew, where did you put my jeweler's box?"

"What jeweler's box?" deadpanned his brother. "Oh, I think Angela was playing with it."

"I was not!" squawked his daughter.

"Daddy's teasing," Cindi assured her.

Andrew patted his pockets. "Say, there is something here. Is this it?" He handed Hugh a small, black velvet box.

"These people are funny," Dr. Archikova said to Tim. "They joke about everything."

"Yeah. Kind of makes you want to punch them in the nose, doesn't it?" he answered, and she laughed.

Meg heard the conversation and, with one part of her mind, enjoyed the give-and-take. Yet she couldn't stop worrying that any minute she was going to wake up. Maybe pinches hurt even when you were dreaming.

All these people couldn't really have come together in a coffee shop transformed with a hodgepodge of holiday decor. And Hugh couldn't be kneeling in front of Meg, opening the box to reveal a beautiful diamond ring.

Instinctively, she touched the simple gold band she'd never stopped wearing since the day three years before when Joe slipped it onto her finger. Once, he'd said, "Someday I'm going to buy you a ring ten times this beautiful."

"Nothing could ever be as beautiful to me," had been her answer.

She'd been wrong. This ring was just as exquisite, because it came from the same loving heart.

Tears spilled down Meg's cheeks. "Don't start crying," Hugh said. "I haven't asked you to marry me yet."

"Yes, you did," she said. "The first time was three years ago."

"I can vouch for that," Sam said. "I heard you."

"No, you didn't!" Hugh challenged. "It was a private conversation."

"You asked her during a work break," Judy confirmed. "You didn't believe anyone could hear you in the hallway, but you were standing by a vent. When you came out afterward, the whole staff applauded."

As they described the event, Hugh chuckled. "You're right. I'd forgotten—no, I mean, it had slipped my mind. Now that you mention it, I remember being glad everybody knew. It meant she couldn't go back on her word."

"As if I would have!" Meg flared.

"So does your acceptance back then mean you have to accept me now?" He quirked one eyebrow hopefully.

"No," she said. "However, I do accept your offer." With all her heart, but she was reluctant to speak so openly in front of a crowd.

"Could we possibly hope for a bit more show of enthusiasm?" Andrew asked.

The standoffish doctor was urging her to become his sister-in-law? "What happened to your suspicions?" Meg asked. "You weren't crazy about me when I showed up in your office."

"I thought you were a fraud," he admitted. "I was wrong. You're good for Hugh."

"Who, I might mention, is waiting down here on the hard floor with his patella—that's kneecap to you laymen—deteriorating," Hugh added. "It's this kind of inconsideration by a man's friends that leads to arthritis in his later years."

"That's a fancy way of encouraging you to say yes," Sam said.

Even though everyone awaited her answer, Meg wasn't inclined to make a show of her feelings. She wanted to get Hugh alone. This was too precious a moment to share with a crowd.

Then she noticed the eager, hopeful expression on Angela's face. The eleven-year-old clearly waited on pins and needles as if for the climax of a favorite movie. She didn't want to miss the good part.

Everyone else wanted to hear more, too, Meg realized. Her father and brother, Hugh's family and the bowling alley buddies all stood silent. They'd worked together to bring about this moment, and they deserved to see the outcome firsthand.

She took a deep breath. "I love you," she said. "I'm sorry I've been so fearful. I was afraid of the future, of change, of not being good enough for you."

"You're definitely good enough for him." Sam winked at Hugh.

"As Dana's mother, you're good enough for anyone," Grace said.

"Meg, you still need to say the magic words." Hugh pressed her hands lightly for emphasis.

"I will." She could hardly speak through the lump in her throat. "I will marry you. Again. And again. However many times it takes to make it stick."

"Yes!" Tim shot his fist into the air triumphantly.

Hugh stood and dusted off his pants. "Unlike most

people, I've led two completely different lives. Today marks the beginning of my real life, because from now on we'll never be separated. Now come here and kiss me."

"Under the holly or in the wedding booth?" Meg asked.

"That isn't a booth, it's a bower," Judy said indignantly.

"It's a booth with a lot of crap on it, that's what it is," came the dry, cracked voice of cafe regular Vinnie Vesputo. Meg hadn't heard the old man enter, but there he stood, eyeing the group as if they'd taken leave of their senses.

"Sir, I'm afraid this is a private party," Sam said, feigning the dignity of an English butler.

"This is a coffee shop and I want my coffee," was the response.

"I'll get it!" To Meg's amusement, Dr. Archikova ducked behind the counter and poured coffee into a cup. "What do you take in it?"

Vinnie seated himself on his usual stool. "The works. Say, have I ever told you my life story?"

"No, and I'd be fascinated," she said.

"You don't happen to be a doctor, do you?" he asked.

"As a matter of fact, I am."

"Good," said Vinnie. "I'm discovering that doctors make the best coffee around here."

Hugh pulled Meg gently against him. "I'll take that kiss now."

"Not with everyone…"

His mouth closed over hers and she forgot what she'd been about to say. It hadn't been important, anyway.

THE PARTY LASTED several hours, with the music on the boom boxes getting louder and everyone helping bring food out of the kitchen. Hugh had never had such a good time in his life.

It was a joy to see the glow on Meg's cheeks. She kept watching him, and then trying to pretend she hadn't been. Joy radiated from her, matching his own.

After the guests left, Sam reopened the cafe, not wanting to disappoint his late-night regulars. Hugh put on a uniform and helped Meg wait tables.

Many of the new arrivals commented on the decor. Others hardly seemed to notice, even when they were offered a slice of oddly colored wedding cake.

"It's a friendly town," Sam explained to Hugh. "Lots of people share their special occasions with whoever stumbles by."

"When are you two actually tying the knot?" Judy asked from beneath a tray of dirty dishes.

Meg and Hugh exchanged glances. "I don't know," she said.

"Soon," he added, reluctant to pressure her but unwilling to wait too long.

"I'd like to keep our original wedding ring," Meg said. "If it's all right with you."

"It's perfect," he said.

Afterward, he walked her to her car. "I'll follow you home, if it's all right."

"Of course it is." Meg leaned against him, small and warm in the early November chill.

"I can move in whenever you say." He didn't care if they ever found a larger place, as long as they were together.

Meg wrapped her arms around him. "Hugh, I've changed my mind."

His heart nearly stopped. No, he thought, she couldn't mean she wasn't going to marry him. "About what?"

"Living in Mercy Canyon." Her eyes were large and dark as she stared up at him in the moonlight. "I don't want you spending so much time on the road. Dana and I will hardly get to see you, and you'll be exhausted."

"I wouldn't have offered if I didn't mean it," he said.

"Of course, if I move to Orange County, I won't be able to keep working," Meg said. "I've been thinking maybe I should go back to school and earn my high school diploma. It would be a good example for Dana."

"If you want to," Hugh said. "I love you the way you are, Meg."

He loved her more than ever tonight, he thought. She'd looked so fragile when she first entered the restaurant that he'd been tempted to grab her and whisk her away.

She was stronger than she appeared, though. She'd risen to the occasion and overcome fears he knew must be deeply rooted. Now she was willing to leave her community, for the sake of their family life.

Meg tightened her grip on him. "I was clinging to the familiar, finding strength in my routines. But security is an illusion. The only one I can really count on is you."

"I won't disappear again," Hugh promised.

"You'd better not." Rising on tiptoe, she kissed him.

He wanted to devour her right here. It was cold, though, and they were standing in a parking lot.

"Home," he said.

"Now," she agreed.

His car followed hers through town in a ball of heat that must surely have raised the town's temperature by a full ten degrees.

ZACK'S FORTY-EIGHTH birthday party, celebrating ten years of sobriety, was held the following weekend in Santa Barbara. Driving there, Meg felt a quiver of alarm as they passed the fateful exit they'd taken more than two years earlier.

Hugh was driving, just as he had been that day. In the back, Dana chattered to her toy hippo.

"It reminds me of…" Meg couldn't finish the sentence.

"The day I vanished?" Hugh said. "It gives me an eerie feeling, too."

She hugged herself. "We were so carefree. I didn't have an inkling that our lives were about to be torn apart."

"I'm sorry we were separated for so long," Hugh said. "I'm glad I got my career and my family back, though."

Meg had spent two desperate years wishing she could undo that scene and return things to the way they'd been. Yet now she was grateful.

Grace and Andrew might have lived the rest of their lives believing he was dead. Dana would never have known her grandmother.

"I'm glad you got them back, too," she said.

"You've had a good effect on my family." Hugh spared her a quick, warm glance. "The Mentons used to keep their emotions under lock and key. You helped us open up."

"We helped each other," Meg said.

"I'll buy that."

A short time later, they arrived in Santa Barbara. Following her father's instructions, Meg directed Hugh through the streets to a whitewashed stucco home surrounded by palm trees. They parked along the circular driveway with a handful of other cars.

She didn't see Tim's aging sedan. "He promised to come," she said. "You heard him."

"I sure did."

She checked her watch. "The party started fifteen minutes ago."

"Fifteen whole minutes and he still isn't here?" Hugh teased. "Maybe we should call the police."

"Oh, you!" She smacked him playfully on the arm before getting out.

Dana, glad to be free of her car seat, insisted on marching across the walkway under her own power. "Independent tyke," Hugh said. "And here you were wondering whether she was old enough to be the flower girl at our wedding."

"I was not!" Meg sputtered.

"I'm sure you mentioned it," he said. "The way you've been talking nonstop about the ceremony."

"I haven't mentioned it once!" Although she knew he was teasing, she sensed a serious undertone to his comments.

All week, Meg had dodged questions about setting a time and place for their wedding. She wasn't sure why.

Since, in her heart, she considered them married already, she had begun moving her possessions into Hugh's apartment and had given Sam notice that she was quitting. So there was no reason not to schedule the ceremony.

Yet something remained missing. The tardiness of her brother today, despite his promise to attend, helped clarify what it was.

Meg wanted her family united. At her first wedding, she'd felt her father's absence keenly. This time, she wanted everyone to come together.

A marriage ceremony had tremendous symbolic meaning. A new life, a new union. For it to be successful, at least in Meg's mind, the loose ends of the old life had to be tied up, the old angers and fears released.

She didn't want tension between her brother and her father. Today was supposed to mark a major step in their reconciliation.

Tim had been acting moody all week, but surely he would come, she told herself. He wasn't really late. There was no reason to worry…yet.

Calligraphy signs directed them along a pathway. They rounded a bend to see a glass-walled studio curving from the back of the house, filled with guests.

As they entered, Hugh indicated the easels and paintings arrayed around the studio. "You can tell an artist lives here."

"It must be a great place to paint." Light spilled into the room, which glowed with the fresh colors of Lynn's watercolors.

Her father and his lady friend came to meet them. "We've been telling everyone there's going to be a wedding in the family soon," Lynn said as she hugged Meg. "I'm so excited."

"The lawyer's still straightening out the paperwork," she said by way of avoiding a direct answer.

At Hugh's suggestion, they had hired an attorney to clear up any questions about the fact that she'd been married before, even though it had been to a husband who technically didn't exist.

"Yes, it might be another thirty seconds or so before he gets finished," Hugh teased.

It was true, Meg conceded silently. The lawyer had assured them there would be no problems.

Lynn whisked them around the room, making introductions. The guests included Zack's co-workers at his shoe store, relatives of Lynn's and numerous artist friends.

The drinks consisted of soft drinks, coffee and non-alcoholic punch. There was a large spread of hors d'oeuvres, more than enough for a meal.

Dana bounced around the room, making friends and eating cheese and crackers. She'd managed to stay awake on the drive, so it was no wonder she began yawning and fell asleep as soon as they tucked her into Lynn's bed.

Half an hour later, Tim arrived. Meg's spirits soared when she saw him, then dipped again when she glimpsed his frown.

Her brother had shed his usual windbreaker for a sports jacket. His shoulders were filling out, she saw, and he stood straighter than usual, like the young man he'd become.

When he shook hands with his father, she saw their eyes meet. Each gave a slight, almost identical nod of recognition, a mannerism that must be hereditary.

"Should we leave them alone together?" Hugh asked.

"It might be awkward," said Lynn, who'd stayed

back to give father and son a little privacy. "Zack's been nervous all week."

"He has?" To Meg, her father looked confident and in complete control.

"He'll never forgive himself for missing your childhoods," Lynn explained. "He knows Tim has good reason to be angry."

"He has even better reasons to make peace," Hugh said. "I can't imagine how unpleasant it must be to live with that kind of resentment."

The two were talking earnestly, Meg saw. She couldn't wait another minute. "I want to find out what they're discussing."

With feigned casualness, she crossed to Zack and Tim. "Hello, you guys." They turned to include her in their circle and she felt a sudden click of connectedness.

"We were discussing your wedding," Zack said.

Meg regarded him wryly. "Fill me in. I'm dying to know the details."

"We didn't mean your dress or the flowers or anything," Tim said. "See, it's been bothering me. At your last wedding, I walked you down the aisle. Now I don't know who ought to do it."

"I can't claim the honor," Zack said. "Although I'd love to if you want."

"I didn't raise you, either," Tim said. "You raised me."

"You've been worrying about this?" she asked in amazement. Of all the things that might trouble her brother, this had never occurred to her.

"Yeah. I've been giving it a lot of thought." His tone was earnest. "I got so distracted while I was driving that I took a wrong turn getting here. Imagine me, a trucker, getting lost!''

"I'm sorry you've been so worried," she said. "You can walk me down the aisle if you want to."

"It would mean a lot to Dad for him to do it," Tim pointed out. "Still, I feel like you and I have kind of a tradition going from last time."

She didn't notice Hugh approaching until he spoke from directly behind her. "Why don't you both do it?"

"Two people walking with her? Wouldn't that be awkward?" Zack asked.

"As I recall, Meg's church has wide aisles," he said.

Tim's face brightened. "I went to a wedding once where the bride's parents both walked with her. What do you think, Dad?"

Zack stared at his son. It was the first time Tim had called him "Dad" since they were children, Meg realized.

Tears sprang into her father's eyes. Struggling against them, Zack cleared his throat. "I'd be honored to walk down the aisle with my two children."

Suddenly Meg couldn't wait for the ceremony. "I'll call the pastor and find out when the church is free."

"I only have one request," Hugh said.

"What?" Meg asked as everyone looked at him with varying degrees of concern.

"Don't let Judy decorate the church," he said.

Chapter Eighteen

From the room where she waited off the foyer, Meg could hear the babble of voices from the church sanctuary. So many people! Even on short notice, everyone had come, from her trailer park friends and the coffee shop staff to Hugh's family and co-workers.

Their two worlds were joined together, as he had promised.

Judy, the matron of honor, and Cindi and Angela, the bridesmaids, clutched their bouquets and waited patiently. Dana played with the basket of rose petals she was to carry up the aisle.

After the ceremony, they would head to the reception in the church hall. For their honeymoon, Meg and Hugh were spending two days at the beach cottage, which was the best they could arrange on such short notice. Next summer, though, they would enjoy a week in Hawaii while Dana stayed with Grace.

Meg was perfectly content. She didn't need an elaborate hotel dinner-dance or any other trappings. It was enough that the man she loved had come back to her.

Tim stuck his head in the door. "We're ready."

When she emerged into the vestibule, Zack was

waiting. Dressed in a tuxedo, her father looked quite distinguished, Meg thought.

"You young ladies go first," he told Angela and Dana, and added a friendly smile for Judy and Cindi. At Thanksgiving dinner a week earlier, when they'd gathered at Grace's house, he'd begun making friends with his new in-laws.

Meg smoothed the simple white skirt of her gown. She'd saved her wedding dress, even though it was far from fancy.

The sentimental value, however, was beyond compare. After Joe's disappearance, Meg had sometimes taken the dress from its protective covering to touch it and remind herself of the happiest day of her life.

How many people got to relive that day in the flesh? she wondered, marveling.

As Dana started down the aisle with Angela behind her, Tim moved into place beside Meg. "You know, Dad and I have a lot in common," he admitted in a low voice. "We both like to fish, we're L.A. Lakers fans and we watch the same TV shows."

"I figured you two would get along if you gave him a chance," she couldn't resist saying.

"In my mind, he was this huge, powerful ogre," her brother said. "After Hugh pointed out that he was about my age when we were born, I started to see him differently. As a person with flaws instead of some all-powerful being."

"Excuse me, did someone mention flaws?" Zack took his place on Meg's other side. "I hope you weren't referring to your beautiful sister."

Tim grinned at his father. "Certainly not!"

"If you meant me, you used the wrong term. What I have aren't flaws, they're boulder-size defects," Zack said. "I can't tell you how lucky I feel that the two of you turned out so well in spite of me."

"You mean I shouldn't ask you for advice someday when I get married and have kids?" Tim asked.

"You can ask all you like," said his father. "Just don't listen to the answers."

From inside the sanctuary, the music switched to "Here Comes the Bride."

"One, two, three, go!" said Zack, and the three of them set forth, arms linked, like the companions in *The Wizard of Oz* heading down the yellow brick road.

"I DO," said Hugh, and slipped the ring on Meg's finger. It was the same ring from before, and the same lovely dress. The happiness on her face was as radiant as it had been, too, although it was suffused with greater wisdom.

They'd been through so much since their first innocent, optimistic wedding day, he thought. Now they'd come around again, richer in understanding and blessed with a daughter, to set out once more on their journey through life.

He could feel Joe watching as he tilted his wife's face and kissed her. Joe stood by his shoulder, sharing the happiness and the memories.

"It is my pleasure to present to you Dr. and Mrs. Hugh Menton," said the same minister who had once introduced them as Mr. and Mrs. Joe Avery.

Applause swept through the church. Among the upturned faces, Hugh picked out his mother's, wet with tears, and Andrew's, his expression pleased.

"Yay! Mom and Dad!" shouted Dana.

From the front row, Grace signaled to her granddaughter. Without hesitation, Dana ran into her arms.

Tucking Meg's hand into his elbow, Hugh escorted her down the aisle. An invisible Joe strode with them. He was happy and hopeful, Hugh sensed, yet a bit uncertain about his place in this new marriage.

They stepped into a side room for a few minutes to let their friends get in place, then emerged into sunshine so bright it washed away shadows. Laughing guests waved soap bubble wands.

Bubbles filled the air, refracting the light into tiny rainbows. All the doubts and delays of the past floated with them and vanished from sight.

"Hurry!" said Meg, laughing. "My hair's getting full of soap."

"Let's go!" Hugh tugged her toward the church hall.

Exhilaration surged inside him as they scampered along the walkway, hand in hand. He was one with the sunshine, one with the woman he loved, one with...

With Joe. The memories and emotions of the past no longer came to Hugh as if from a distance. In the last few minutes, his other self had melted into him.

He and Joe had one heart, one personality, one future and one woman to love. The years of confusion and displacement were over.

Joe Avery, lost for so long, had come home.

There's a baby on the way!

Harlequin truly does
make any time special. . . .
This year we are celebrating
weddings in style!

A
Walk
Down
the Aisle
WEDDING CELEBRATION

To help us celebrate, we want you to tell us how wearing the Harlequin wedding gown will make your wedding day special. As the grand prize, Harlequin will offer one lucky bride the chance to **"Walk Down the Aisle"** in the Harlequin wedding gown!

There's more...

For her honeymoon, she and her groom will spend five nights at the **Hyatt Regency Maui.** As part of this five-night honeymoon at the hotel renowned for its romantic attractions, the couple will enjoy a candlelit dinner for two in Swan Court, a sunset sail on the hotel's catamaran, and duet spa treatments.

A HYATT RESORT AND SPA

Maui • Molokai • Lanai

To enter, please write, in, 250 words or less, how wearing the Harlequin wedding gown will make your wedding day special. The entry will be judged based on its emotionally compelling nature, its originality and creativity, and its sincerity. This contest is open to Canadian and U.S. residents only and to those who are 18 years of age and older. There is no purchase necessary to enter. Void where prohibited. See further contest rules attached. Please send your entry to:

Walk Down the Aisle Contest

In Canada	In U.S.A.
P.O. Box 637	P.O. Box 9076
Fort Erie, Ontario	3010 Walden Ave.
L2A 5X3	Buffalo, NY 14269-9076

You can also enter by visiting www.eHarlequin.com
Win the Harlequin wedding gown and the vacation of a lifetime!
The deadline for entries is October 1, 2001.

HARLEQUIN®
Makes any time special ®